"D

"I mean, are you enjoying what's happening between you and me?" Juliet's voice was soft, hesitant.

"Hell, yes," Cody answered.

"Then what...what's wrong?"

"I didn't say anything was wrong, exactly."

"Then why can't we just...enjoy this?"

"We are. I am. That isn't the point. I want to talk, that's all."

She looked at him, her expression desperate and unhappy. Finally she pleaded, "Can't we just wait? Please?"

"Until when?"

She sighed. "Until the festival's over. Can't we just have a wonderful time until then?"

"Live out your fantasy, you mean?" His voice had a bitter edge.

She looked away. "Yes. I suppose."

He was quiet, considering. He was her fantasy-come-true, and nothing more. Soon enough, she'd be ready for reality again—and he'd be out the door....

Dear Reader,

Joan Hohl is back! And I know you're all cheering at her return. Her *Man of the Month* book, *Convenient Husband,* is Joan at her steamiest, and her hero, Jasper (also known as "Main") Chance, is a man to remember. That's *all* I'm going to tell you about this sexy, sensuous story.... You'll just have to read it for yourself.

A book by Lass Small is always a treat, and you'll all be thrilled to know that *A Restless Man* is the first in her three-book series about those Fabulous Brown Brothers. (Yes, you first met Bob Brown in her 1991 *Man of the Month* book, *'Twas the Night.*) Look for more of the Brown men in October and December.

August is completed with a terrific story from Mary Lynn Baxter, *And Baby Makes Perfect* (another hero to remember!); *Just Like Old Times* by Jennifer Greene (watch out for the matchmaking teenagers!); *Midsummer Madness* by Christine Rimmer (with Cody McIntyre, town hunk); and *Sarah and the Stranger* by Shawna Delacorte, a new author you'll hear more of.

Next month, look for Silhouette Desire books by some of your favorite authors, including Annette Broadrick, Diana Palmer and Helen R. Myers.

All the best,

Lucia Macro
Senior Editor

CHRISTINE RIMMER

MIDSUMMER MADNESS

SILHOUETTE *Desire*®

Published by Silhouette Books New York
America's Publisher of Contemporary Romance

SILHOUETTE BOOKS
300 East 42nd St., New York, N.Y. 10017

MIDSUMMER MADNESS

ISBN: 0-373-05729-6

First Silhouette Books printing August 1992

Books by Christine Rimmer

Silhouette Desire

No Turning Back #418
Call It Fate #458
Temporary Temptress #602
Hard Luck Lady #640
Midsummer Madness #729

Silhouette Special Edition

Double Dare #646
Slow Larkin's Revenge #698
Earth Angel #719

CHRISTINE RIMMER,

a third generation Californian, came to her profession the long way around. Before settling down to write about the magic of romance, she'd been an actress, a sales clerk, a janitor, a model, a phone sales representative, a teacher, a waitress, a playwright and an office manager. Now that she's finally found work that suits her perfectly, she insists she never had a problem keeping a job—she was merely gaining "life experience" for her future as a novelist. Those who know her best withhold comment when she makes such claims; they are grateful that she's at last found steady work. Christine is grateful, too—not only for the joy she finds in writing, but for what waits when the day's work is through: a man she loves who loves her right back, and the privilege of watching their children grow and change day to day.

For my sister, B. J. Jordan,
who always believed in me,
and for my brother, Paul Smith,
who held out a hand when I needed one

One

—

"Cody, um, I'll take over... if you want...."

Cody McIntyre didn't hear the hesitant proposition, partly because it was spoken so softly, and partly because he was glaring at the phone he'd just slammed back into its cradle. His mind was occupied with dark, murderous thoughts—thoughts that concerned the immediate and permanent elimination from the world of the "expert" from Hollywood who was supposed to have shown up in Emerald Gap the day before, and who had just called to say he wasn't going to be showing up at all.

"Cody...."

This time he heard something. "Hmm?" he asked absently, glancing at the only other person in the room, his bookkeeper, Juliet Huddleston, whom he'd known all his life. Juliet sat at the spare desk in the corner, with his mid-month payroll spread out in front of her. "You say something, Julie?"

Maybe he really should sue the bastard, Cody was thinking, though lawsuits were generally not his style. Men like Cody considered a handshake a bond—and simply cut off dealings with people who didn't.

Juliet sat on an armless swivel chair. Now she spun in the chair, until she faced him straight on. "I said, I'll do it."

Cody hadn't the faintest idea what she was talking about, but he figured it must be important. She was looking directly at him, her hazel eyes unwavering. For shy Julie Huddleston, a dead-on look like the one she was giving him was such a rarity as to be kind of spooky.

"You all right, Julie?"

"I'm fine." She straightened her narrow shoulders and tugged on the jacket of the gray business suit she was wearing. "And I want to do it." She looked downright resolute.

"Er, do what?"

She cleared her throat. "I want to take over that director's job. I want to run the town pageant this year."

Cody stared at her, his surprise at what she'd just proposed so complete that he more or less forgot how to talk for a moment. Then his voice returned. "Midsummer Madness?" He muttered the name of the annual ten-day festival in frank disbelief. "*You* want to run Midsummer Madness this year?"

Juliet picked up his amazement at her suggestion, and blinked. She suddenly looked more like herself. Her eyes got that soft, anxious look. But she didn't give in. She confirmed, "Yes," the affirmative weakened only by the little gasp she took between the *y* and the *e*.

Cody stole a moment to comb his hair back with his fingers. He liked Julie, always had. In fact, ever since they were kids, he'd always made it a point to keep one eye out for her. The last thing he wanted to do was disappoint her; she was such a gentle soul.

But the Juliet Huddlestons of the world were not festival directors, not by a long shot. Once again, he silently cursed the delinquent professional he'd hired, this time for making it necessary for him to hurt poor Julie's feelings.

Cody regretfully shook his head. "That's sweet of you, Julie. But we've got to face facts. Running a pageant isn't really up your alley."

Cody watched the hopeful light fade from her eyes and felt like a rat for putting it out. Her shoulders fell, and she slowly turned back to the open check register and the stack of time cards on the desk.

Cody started around his own desk, to get closer to her and ease her hurt feelings a little. But he was stopped by the knock on the door.

"It's open," he called.

The door was flung back, and the room was filled with the sounds from the busy kitchen outside. Cody's office was behind McIntyre's, the bar and grill he owned and operated himself. He also owned and managed the hardware store down the street, and the family ranch a few miles out of town. Cody was a busy man. Too busy, he thought again, to run the damn summer pageant himself this year. But that was exactly what he was going to be doing.

Each of the merchants in town took a turn, and this year was his. He'd thought it a stroke of brilliance to convince them to bring in an expert. So much for brilliance. So much for damn experts....

"Here you are, you devil. The bartender said I could find you back here." The shapely brunette in the doorway to the kitchen wore painted-on jeans and a little-girl pout. "Remember me?"

Cody's mama had raised him right. He tried to be tactful, in spite of the fact that he couldn't recollect ever seeing this woman before in his life. "Pardon me, but I don't recall where we met before, ma'am." Over the woman's shoulder, he could see the day pot washer, Elroy, paused in midscrub and leering suggestively. "Why don't you just come on in and close that door?" Cody suggested.

The woman made a big production of shutting the door. She glanced once in Juliet's direction, and then shrugged, apparently deciding to pretend Julie wasn't there. Next, the woman leaned against the closed door and sighed, a move which displayed her generous breasts to distinct advantage. "I kept hoping you'd call."

"Excuse me, but who are you?"

"God, you are one gorgeous hunk of man."

"Ma'am. Won't you tell me your name?"

"Lorena. I wrote it on that matchbook that I gave to the waitress with the red hair. Last Saturday, it was. You sang that Garth Brooks song. I was at that itty-bitty table, way in the back corner. I had a date. But I whispered to that waitress to explain to you that I was a totally free woman, ready, willing, and able to get to know a terrifically incredible guy like yourself—"

"So then we've never met before, ma'am?"

At the small desk in the corner, Juliet couldn't help but hear all this. She stifled a small, sympathetic smile and almost forgot her own problems as she tried to block out the sound of poor Cody dealing with another avid admirer.

"Well, we haven't met formally, of course," the brunette allowed. "But come on, admit it, you saw me back there. Don't try to hide it from me. You felt it, too, when our eyes collided. Bam. Like a jolt. A bolt out of the blue."

"Well, ma'am. I can't precisely say that what you're describing happened for me...."

Juliet shook her head. Poor Cody. The women just wouldn't leave him alone. He had a talent with a harmonica and a guitar. He also had a slow, sexy singing voice and sometimes even wrote his own songs. When the mood struck, on occasional weekends, he'd sing a few numbers in the bar out front. That drove the ladies wild.

Also, besides being a talented musician and singer, Cody McIntyre just happened to be drop-dead gorgeous—in a very manly sort of way.

"Honey—" the brunette put a hand on her hip and sighed again "—I can *make* it happen for you. You just give me a chance...." She looked at Cody as if she longed to gobble him alive.

Objectively, Juliet could understand the brunette's desire. Most women felt the same way when they looked at Cody. He could have been the prince in a grown-up woman's fairy tale.

His shining gray-green eyes, with whites so white they dazzled, looked out from under straight brows. His nose was perfectly symmetrical, with nostrils that flared just enough to show sensitivity, but not enough to make a woman doubt his ability to take charge. His mouth was a sculpture, firm yet responsive, with the engaging tendency to curl with humor on the right side. His chin was strong, but not too square. His hair was brown with golden highlights. His ears did not stick out. And most important for a handsome man, he really didn't seem to care a bit about how he looked.

And on top of all that, he was a genuinely good person.

As the brunette went on leaning against the door and sighing with great enthusiasm, Juliet filled out another check and tried to mind her own business.

She didn't entirely succeed. From thoughts of how poor Cody couldn't keep the women at bay, she found herself deciding that there was a certain similarity between herself and him.

Strange. She herself was the invisible woman, so plain and bland that everyone—men especially—saw right through her. And Cody McIntyre was a living, breathing masculine dream. Yet he lived alone as she did, having failed so far to find the right woman among all the ladies who threw themselves at his feet. Sometimes lately, Juliet found herself feeling more sorry for him than for herself.

Correction, Juliet thought, shaking a mental finger at herself. I do *not* feel sorry for myself. Not anymore. I've taken the reins of my life in my own two hands now. And I'm making the next thirty years more exciting than the past thirty were, or I will die trying.

Such was Juliet Titania Huddleston's birthday resolution. She'd made the vow just four months before, on the day she hit the big three-oh. She'd told no one, partly because no one asked, and partly because this was her own private project, her business alone.

Juliet had already taken some specific steps to make her resolution a reality. And she intended to keep taking steps, until she had reached her goal.

Juliet straightened in her chair at just the idea of her vow. At that moment, the shapely brunette sashayed across the room to Cody's desk, trailing an insistent cloud of musky perfume.

"So what do you say, darlin'?" the woman breathed. "How 'bout you, me, a bottle of wine and a big, fat full moon?"

Cody kindly demurred, and then ushered the woman back toward the door. With a gentle skill born of extensive experience, he had the woman out the door and on her way before she even realized she'd been turned down.

Juliet was busily filling out the final check when a shadow fell across the paper.

"Julie?"

She looked up into Cody's beautiful and sympathetic eyes—and made one of those wimpy little questioning sounds she'd been making all her life.

Inside, Juliet groaned at her own ingrained meekness. But then she gamely reminded herself that no one got assertive overnight. Little by little, she'd eliminate everything wimpy from her life, but she wasn't going to be too hard on herself if she backslid now and then.

"Are you going to be all right?" Cody was asking.

Juliet knew what he was talking about. He wanted to be sure she had accepted the fact that directing Midsummer Madness was not a job for her.

Juliet considered. She had to admit that he was probably right. The truth was, she'd never directed anything in her life. And telling other people what to do was something for which she'd yet to show the slightest aptitude. Some people are born to lead; they shine in the limelight. And some are born to sit in the background, tallying receipts. Juliet knew quite well into which category she fell. She opened her mouth to tell him she understood why he didn't want to give her a chance.

But something inside her choked the words off before they took form. There was her birthday vow to remember. If she hungered for more out of life than she'd had so far, she simply had to get out there and take what she wanted.

She decided she just wasn't willing to give up on this yet. "I . . . I can do it, Cody. Let me try."

Cody's expression turned pained. He ambled away and hitched a leg up on the corner of his desk. He looked down at the rawhide boot on his dangling foot. "Now, Julie," he said, still studying his boot. "I'd say you haven't really given this notion much thought."

"I h-have, too. Give me a chance."

He looked up from his boot and into her eyes. His face spoke of great patience, and even greater conviction that she was asking to take on more than someone like her could ever hope to handle.

Juliet looked right back at him and found herself experiencing a truly alien emotion for someone as terminally timid as she'd always been.

The emotion was annoyance. He didn't have to be so utterly certain that her running the pageant would be a disaster. Maybe leadership wasn't her strong suit, but she did have some of the necessary qualities, after all. She'd earned a four-year degree and managed her own bookkeeping business, so she possessed the requisite organizational skills. And she'd been involved with the pageant, in minor capacities, almost every year of her life. She knew what needed to be done.

"Julie," Cody said then, still in that infinitely understanding tone. "Be realistic. You'd have to oversee the entire opening-day parade, not to mention plan the Gold Rush Ball and direct the Midsummer Madness Revue. How are you going to manage all that, when most of the time I have to ask twice just to hear what you said?"

Juliet felt her shoulders start to slump again. He was right. She couldn't do it. Not a timid mouse like her. Not in a million years....

Hey, wait a minute here, that new woman deep inside herself argued. Who took that weekend assertiveness training retreat last month and came out of it with a new awareness of how to know what she wants and take steps to get it? Who's been going to Toastmasters International in secret since April, driving all the way to Auburn every Friday night in order to conquer her fear of public speaking? Who's stood up there and spoken before the group three times in the past two months, achieving a higher score each time?

Me, Juliet, that's who.

"I can speak up," she said aloud, "if I force myself. I've been working on that."

Cody, for his part, was studying her, puzzled why shy Julie would even consider taking on such a task, let alone insist on it. Then it came to him how to settle this problem once and for all.

He lowered his dangling foot to the floor and stood up. "All right, then," he said, seeming to give in to her.

She blinked. "You agree? You'll let me handle it?"

"It's not my decision."

"What do you mean?"

"I mean—" he shrugged "—that you can talk to the merchants' association at seven tonight." The words were offhand, though he knew they'd have a crushing effect. Julie would never get up in front of a group of people and give a speech. Now she would have no choice but to back down.

Cody began a casual circuit of his desk, not looking at her anymore. There was dead silence from Juliet's corner of the room. He was positive she'd be wearing that stricken look she got when anyone even suggested she do something that might draw attention to herself. He'd always hated to see that look on her face, because he knew it meant she was suffering agonies of shyness.

However, a little suffering now was preferable to her getting too carried away with this crazy idea that she could take over Midsummer Madness for that damned delinquent expert from Hollywood.

Cody continued in an offhand tone. "You can impress them all with what a great idea it would be to hire you. I mean, you might as well start forcing yourself to speak up right away, don't you think?"

Cody reached his leather chair and plunked himself down in it. He allowed a benign smile, confident that he'd handled this little predicament just right. Faced with the prospect of getting up in front of all those people, shy Julie would run the other way quicker than a cat with its tail on fire.

He looked directly at her again, steeling himself for the agony he'd see on her face, and for the defeated expression that would come next. It took him several seconds to absorb what he actually saw.

Her chin was set, her lips pressed together. She looked— by God, she looked determined. When she spoke, Cody couldn't believe his ears.

"All right," she said. "I'll speak to the merchants' association at seven tonight."

Two

"And, as for the Midsummer Madness Revue," Juliet announced in a calm, clear voice, "well, I just think we can have a lot of fun with it this year. We'll have music by the Barbershop Boys and the school choirs, as always. And I also think maybe I could line up a few of our local favorites to give us a number or two. There'll be poems by Flat-nosed Jake." Juliet winked at Jake, a bearded, scruffy character in the front row, whose nose appeared to have collided with something unyielding at some point in his life. "Jake, as most of you know, is poet emeritus of our fair city. And we'll include a skit detailing the settlement of Emerald Gap by a group of prospectors back in 1852. Also, Melda Cooks has written a reenactment of the hanging of Maria Elena Roderica Perez Smith, who, as you might recall, was a local laundress lynched here after she stabbed a man to death in a brawl in the spring of 1856...."

At the back of Emerald Gap Auditorium, where the bright spill of light that shone on Juliet's pale hair did not reach, Cody sat in one of the creaky old theater seats and wondered what the hell was going on.

What had happened to shy Julie Huddleston?

This afternoon, no sooner had she knocked his boots off by saying she'd speak before the merchants' association, than she'd demanded all the planning materials he'd been saving to give to the pro from Hollywood. With the big folder tucked safely under her arm, she'd taken right off for her own small office two blocks away.

She must have gotten right on the phone, because all the people she was claiming were going to help her out were sitting down front now, nodding and smiling and looking like they were willing to follow her off the nearest cliff if she asked them to.

And why the hell not? Her start had been a little rocky— that much was true. She'd had that freaky spooked rabbit look for just a minute there when she got behind that podium and realized all those faces were staring at her. But she'd recovered—boy, had she. She'd recovered just fine.

Up on the stage, Juliet continued. "And, since this is gold country after all, I think the ball on Saturday, the third, should be a genuinely gala event. This year we'll really put some effort into making it a true costume affair, talk as many locals as possible into dressing in the period. . . ."

Back in the darkness, Cody shook his head. On the one hand, he was experiencing a massive feeling of relief because it looked like the association was going to hire Julie to do the job. Cody was going to be let off the hook for it.

On the other hand, though, he felt a kind of creeping disquiet. He looked at Julie up there in the light, and he wondered if he knew her at all.

Which was crazy. He'd known her practically all his life. They were the same age and had gone through school together.

Cody smiled to himself, remembering Julie on the first day of kindergarten. The teacher, Miss Oakleaf, had called the roll. And Julie had been too scared to say her name. She'd stared down at her lap, her white skin flushing painful red, her little hands shaking.

In his memory, Julie had always been like that—afraid of her own shadow, keeping to herself, quivering visibly at any notice paid to her. He'd been a little surprised that she got through state college, wondered how she'd survived the crowds. But she'd done it, and she'd returned to Emerald Gap to set up her own business, with herself as her only employee. He'd hired her right off, and so had half of the other merchants and small businessmen in town. She was doing well, but always in that quiet, retiring way that she had. At least until recently.

Cody made a low sound in his throat, as it occurred to him that for the past few weeks Julie had been driving around in a red sports car. He'd seen the red car, on a morning when he'd gone out to do the chores, parked in front of the guesthouse at his ranch. Her little brown economy car had been nowhere in sight.

And that was another thing. Three months ago, he'd decided to rent out the guesthouse. Julie had taken it. It had never crossed his mind to question why she would suddenly decide to move out of the big house in town that her parents had left to her when they retired, and into a two-bedroom cottage fifteen miles from most of her clients; he'd simply been glad to get someone dependable so easily. But now he wondered....

Not that he was likely, the way things were, to find out much. They lived less than three hundred yards from each other, yet it might as well be three hundred miles; they each maintained strict privacy.

Up on the stage, Julie laughed. It was a shy little laugh, but a charming one. Her pale hair, which was straight and hung to her shoulders, had a smooth, curried sheen in the flood of light from above.

Cody shifted in the seat, trying to accommodate his long legs more comfortably without doing what he longed to do—swing his boots up on the row in front of him. Andrea Oakleaf, still very much a schoolteacher, was down in the second row. If she turned and saw him with his boots up, he'd be hearing about it in no uncertain terms.

Juliet made a mild joke. A ripple of laughter passed through the hall.

She was definitely changing, Cody thought. His efficient yet touchingly bashful bookkeeper wasn't so bashful anymore. What could have made her decide to step out of the shadows after all these years?

Maybe, he thought, he should ask her out to dinner sometime and find out. After all, they were friends, weren't they? There couldn't be any harm in spending an evening or two enjoying each other's company. They could laugh over old times together and really get to know each other—

Cody straightened up and cut off the rambling thought.

What the hell was going on here? He'd been wondering what was happening with Julie. Maybe a better question would be, what was happening with *him?* Why the big interest in a woman who'd been around since they were both in diapers?

Cody decided not to think about that. It was no big deal. He'd put thoughts of Julie—and thoughts about why he was thinking so much about Julie—right out of his mind.

That decided, he focused on the stage again—and saw Julie.

All at once, unable to sit still, he swung his boots up on the back of the chair in front of him, recalled Miss Oakleaf, and swung them back down again. They hit the old pine strip floor a mite too firmly, and Andrea Oakleaf turned briefly around to shoot one of her famous squinty-eyed looks toward the darkness where he sat. After that, Cody kept his feet on the floor and his mind, more or less, in control.

Up on the stage, Juliet finished her speech. She left the podium to the accompaniment of approving applause. She sat, feeling as if she floated there, on a folding chair to the left of the podium, while questions were asked of her. She had answers to all of them.

It was incredible.

Melda Cooks asked how Juliet would handle casting the play she'd written. Juliet remembered past years, when they'd had tryouts, and no one had shown up. Or when they'd cast by asking around, and some people had felt left out.

So Juliet said she'd combine the two methods: a day of tryouts, and then any uncast roles would be filled by appealing to the community consciousness of people who might fit the parts. Juliet raised her eyebrows just a fraction when she said "community consciousness," and everyone chuckled a little. They all knew what she meant; they'd end up begging a few softhearted souls to get involved.

Babe Allen pointedly remarked that Juliet could hardly expect to be paid what they'd agreed to pay the expert from Hollywood. Juliet, prepared for that one, smiled sweetly and answered that she was willing to do the work as a community service—provided the merchants donated the full fee they would have paid to the new community park down at the foot of Commercial Street.

It was so...marvelously simple. And *fun.* She just used her head, and then explained what she'd figured out, and it made sense. People listened. Amazing. Wonderful.

After they took the vote and elected her, Juliet approached the podium again to murmur a brief thank-you and to ask her committee heads—whom she'd lined up just this afternoon—to confer with her briefly in the lobby after the meeting was over. Then she gathered up her materials and left the stage through the wings, floating out the stage door, and then circling around to wait for the others in the quiet lobby out front.

Within a half hour, all her people were assembled. Jake, who was not only a poet but also worked part-time on the *Emerald Gap Bulletin,* agreed to get right on the posters and newspaper notice for the revue tryouts, which would be held on Monday evening. Reva Reid, parade committee chairman, would make the rounds tomorrow to firm up the list of all the floats and themes. The frog jump and Race Day chairpeople respectively agreed that they'd have each event fully planned by Tuesday evening, when the pageant committee would meet once again. Andrea Oakleaf volunteered to check with the Pine Grove Park Commission about the permit for the big closing-day picnic. And Burt Pandley promised to find, by next Friday, at least twelve more participants for the Crafts and Industry Fair, which was slated to run upstairs in the town hall the whole ten days of the festival.

It was after nine when Juliet finally left the lobby of the old auditorium. Outside, the night was balmy and moonless, the air very still. She stood for a moment beyond the big entry doors, between a pair of Victorian gas street lamps, and shivered just a little with excitement and triumph. She drew a deep breath and thought she could smell the pines and firs that cloaked the surrounding foothills.

How beautiful Broad Street looked, clothed in night, with its brick-fronted buildings, and the old-fashioned gas lamps all along the street. On the corner diagonally across from her, she could see the lights in the window of Cody's restaurant.

Now where, she wondered suddenly, had Cody disappeared to? He'd been waiting for her in the front row when she first entered the auditorium tonight. He'd wished her luck and then taken the podium for a moment to explain about the loss of the professional from Hollywood. He'd introduced her and left the stage.

And then she'd forgotten all about him in the excitement—and terror—of getting up and making herself heard.

Juliet grinned. Well, she'd see him soon enough. Between the work she did for him and the fact that she lived on his ranch, they ran into each other almost daily.

It was going to be fun, she decided, to tease him about not believing in her. He'd be a little embarrassed, she knew, and he'd smile that beautiful right-sided smile....

Juliet shivered a little, though the windless, warm night didn't justify goose bumps. Odd, that she should think about teasing Cody. She wasn't a teasing type of person, really.

Or she hadn't been. But now, with what she'd accomplished tonight, Juliet was beginning to think that she could be just about any kind of person she wanted to be.

And if she wanted to tease a friend a little, why shouldn't she? There was nothing wrong with that....

"Great job, Juliet."

Juliet jumped, like someone caught thinking naughty thoughts. "Oh." She gave a guilty giggle. "You surprised me, Jake."

Flat-nosed Jake's squashed face wrinkled with amusement. "*You* surprised all of *us*, gal. Damn good show."

"Well, thank you."

"Thank *you*," Jake said. "We can use a real leader around here for once."

"I'll do my best."

Nodding, Jake turned and strolled off down the street toward the ancient green pickup he'd been driving for as long as Juliet could remember.

Juliet stood for a moment more, savoring Jake's praise, staring at a street she'd known all her life, but which tonight seemed the most beautiful place on earth. And then she turned and headed for McIntyre's, because she'd parked her car just a few feet beyond the restaurant's doors.

When she reached her car, Juliet paused once again, as she had outside the auditorium. She gazed fatuously at the automobile. It was a night to feel good about herself, and the car just added to the wonderfulness of it all.

Low, long, and sleek, it was the color of a scarlet flame. The salesman had told her it had eight cylinders, which he had implied was plenty, and which she suspected was probably immoral these days. She certainly felt immoral whenever she bought gas, which was often. It was not a practical car, nor was it precisely new—it had had one owner before her, who'd put quite a few miles on it, actually. But the salesman had assured her that the car was in tip-top condition. And she hadn't bought it for practical reasons, anyway.

She'd seen it and wanted it, and now it was hers. For Juliet, the car was a symbol, a material representation of the way she was creating a whole new life for herself. So she looked at it awhile, on this special night-of-all-nights, and thought it was the most beautiful thing she'd ever laid eyes on in her life.

Still floating on air from her triumph with the merchants' association, Juliet shrugged out of the gray jacket that went with her suit. She tossed the jacket and her pageant materials in back and slid beneath the wheel. The car was so low and streamlined that Juliet almost felt as if she were lying down when she settled into the driver's seat. It was a glorious feeling.

Stretching out, sighing a little, she rolled down the window and unbuttoned the top two buttons of her white cotton blouse. The warm night air came in the window and kissed her throat.

Sensuous, Juliet thought. Downright sensuous, just sitting here.

And then she giggled. Sensuous. What a thought. Especially for plain-Jane Juliet Huddleston, who was getting real close to being considered a spinster by everyone in town.

The warm air played on blushing skin now, as Juliet rather primly reminded herself that everyone had sexy thoughts now and then, even thirty-year-old virgins who probably ought to know better.

But then, why *should* she know better? A woman who could do what she'd done tonight was no doubt perfectly capable of removing all her clothes and having an intimate experience with a man.

Eventually.

. . . Given that he was the *right* man, of course.

As she sat up enough to stick the key in the ignition, Juliet considered what the right man might be like.

He'd be good and kind and funny. A steady man, who, like herself, would never waver in his devotion. An attractive man—but not too attractive. Juliet was a realist, after all. She wanted, when the time came, a man to last a lifetime. And really good-looking men—men like Cody, for instance—were forever being tempted by one woman after another.

Juliet turned the key that she'd stuck in the ignition, and then forgot all about her mental shopping list for the ideal man. Because something strange happened when she turned the key, something totally unexpected: nothing. The car didn't start.

Juliet checked to see that she was in neutral. She was. She shifted it out and then back into neutral again, just to be sure. Then she turned the key again.

And again, it didn't start.

So she popped the hood latch and went to look at the engine. Which told her exactly zero. Juliet knew nothing about cars, except how to drive them and where to put the gas.

She did notice, however, that it didn't look quite so spanking clean under the hood as it had when she'd bought the car three weeks ago. There appeared to be oil leaking out in some places. She thought that strange.

"Got a problem?"

Juliet sighed in relief at the sound of the familiar voice. Cody. As always, when Juliet had a problem, Cody just naturally seemed to appear to help her out.

She removed her head from beneath the hood and shyly smiled at him. "Hi." Her voice did that funny wimpy thing, between the *h* and the *i*, that little hitching sound, but she didn't let it bother her. She went on, more strongly. "My car won't start."

For a minute, he just stood there and looked at her. It was odd. She wondered if she had engine oil on her nose or something. She was just about to ask what was wrong, when he added, as if he thought he should explain, "Saw you from the window." He gestured in the general direction of his restaurant.

She said, "Oh," and thought about how she'd leaned back in the seat and unbuttoned her blouse and imagined taking off her clothes for a man. Had he watched her through all that? She felt her face flushing.

Which was ridiculous. Even if Cody *had* been watching her the whole time—which she was sure he hadn't—what was wrong with leaning back in the seat and loosening her collar? Nothing. What she had been thinking was her own business. He could know nothing of that.

They kept on looking at each other. She wondered about something she'd never wondered about before: What was Cody thinking?

She opened her mouth, planning to ask him what was on his mind and be done with it, when he seemed to shake himself. He blinked and said, "Want me to have a look?"

She almost asked, "At what?" but then remembered. Her car. He would look at her car.

"Yes. Great. Thanks."

He stuck his head beneath the hood and fiddled with a few of the wires. He took a few caps off of various doo-hickies in there.

"Battery's not dry," he muttered. "Nothing seems to have come unhooked." He leaned out toward her where she stood on the sidewalk. "Get in and try it again."

She did as he'd asked. And once more, nothing happened. He fiddled some more under the hood, she tried starting it once more, but still nothing happened.

After the third try, he said, "Was it giving you trouble before this?"

"No, none at all."

"Just now, did it turn over at all the first time you tried it?"

She shook her head.

"You got nothing, not even a groaning sound?"

"Not a thing."

"Then it's probably not your battery. Maybe it's just a loose connection, or possibly your starter. Hell, it could be a hundred things." He took a handkerchief from a pocket and wiped his hands on it. "Tell you what, I'm heading back to the ranch now, anyway. Why don't you ride home with me? You can call the garage in the morning."

Juliet, worried about her beloved car, shook her head. "Do you think it's anything serious?"

"That it won't start . . . ? Probably not. But these gaskets look shot, and the seals don't seem to be holding."

"What does that mean?"

He gave her a look with way too much patience in it to be reassuring. Then he asked, "Where'd you buy this car, Julie?"

"Don's Hot Deals, outside of Auburn."

"How much did you pay for it?"

She told him.

He looked pained. "I've always thought of you as practical, before this."

"I know." She giggled, forgetting altogether that she was not a giggling kind of person. She added, downright pertly, "There are a lot of things about me that aren't the way they used to be."

"I noticed."

He looked at her some more, and she looked back. It was kind of fun, Juliet thought, these long pauses where they just looked at each other. At least, it was fun for her. Looking at Cody McIntyre was a purely pleasurable pastime.

"How much do you owe on it?" he asked eventually.

"The car?"

"Yeah."

"Not a cent. I paid cash."

"Hell, Julie."

Juliet smiled and shrugged. "I wanted it. So I bought it."

"You still have that little brown car?"

"Nope. I never want to see a brown car again."

Cody shook his head. "Come on. Let's not stand here all night. Get your things and let's go home."

Juliet got her jacket and the big manila folder and followed Cody to his shiny black pickup in the lot behind McIntyre's.

They were quiet as Cody pulled out of the lot and headed for the edge of town. But once they'd left the lights of Emerald Gap behind and begun the twenty-minute ride to the McIntyre ranch, Cody had a suggestion. "You can use my spare pickup, if you want, until you get that car fixed."

She looked over at him, smiling. "You're so good to me, Cody. You always have been. Don't think I haven't noticed."

He looked a little embarrassed at that, and spent a few moments paying great attention to the road. Then he said gruffly, "I've got to be honest, Julie. I think you bought yourself a world of headaches with that car."

Juliet sighed. "I love it, anyway. I'll get it fixed, that's all." She was a little worried about the car. But tonight, even the possibility that she'd spent several thousand dollars on a bona fide lemon didn't daunt her. Nothing could faze her tonight.

Because she, Juliet Huddleston, who'd spent her whole life in the background taking orders rather than giving them, was going to run Midsummer Madness this year! The prospect was terrifying, but exhilarating, as well.

She rolled down the window and let the warm wind blow back her hair. Then she turned to Cody, ready to tease him a little as she'd imagined doing a while before.

"You didn't stick around to congratulate me."

He chuckled. "After the meeting, you were occupied in the lobby. I figured I'd see you soon enough, and you could give me a hard time about my lack of faith in you."

"Why, Cody McIntyre. When in our lives have I ever given you a hard time?"

He threw her a glance. "When have you ever led a festival? Or owned a red car? Or rented your big house in town, to move out in the sticks?"

"It is not the sticks," she reproved him. "It is the McIntyre ranch, where I have longed to live ever since first grade when your mom gave that pool party the last day of school. And now I *do* live there."

He didn't laugh this time, but there was humor in his voice when he said, "I get it. Living in my guesthouse is the fulfillment of a lifelong dream."

"Not exactly. Not quite so permanent as a dream. More temporary. Like a fantasy."

He grunted. "As your landlord, I'm bound to ask, exactly how *temporary* do you mean?"

"Oh, Cody. Don't worry. I'll give a month's notice before I leave. And it won't be for a year or two, at least. What I mean is, it's just something I always wanted to do, not something that lasts a lifetime. That's all."

He was quiet for a time, digesting this. Then he said, "So what gives, Julie?"

His serious tone surprised her. She answered in her old way, with that little frightened catch. "Wh-what do you mean?"

"You're different. You've changed. I didn't really notice it until today, when you suddenly insisted I let you take on the pageant. But it's been happening for a while, a few months at least. I can see that now, looking back on things."

She turned in her seat to face him. He gave her a quick, encouraging smile. Then he looked back at the road, which was climbing now, up into the pines, as they grew nearer the ranch. "I'd really like to know, Julie," he said, this time not glancing over.

"Y-you would?"

He nodded.

She realized she wanted to tell him. Maybe it was that he'd actually asked; no one had asked before. Or maybe her confidence was finally high enough, that after tonight, she wouldn't need to keep her resolution secret anymore.

But she supposed it didn't really matter why. What mattered was he'd asked.

As he drove the twisting road to the ranch, she told him everything. About her vow that her next thirty years were going to amount to more than the past thirty had—and about all the steps she'd taken to make that vow come true.

He listened and nodded, and laughed a little when she told about that first time up in front of the group at Toastmasters International, when she'd been so nervous that she'd gestured wildly, knocking over her water glass into her shoes, which then made embarrassing squishing sounds every time she shifted her weight through the rest of her speech.

The miles flew by. She was just telling him how terrified she'd been for those first seconds up on the stage this evening, when the front entrance to the ranch came into sight. It was a high stone wall broken by two widely spaced stone pillars, with an iron *M* on a rocker in a cast-iron arch across the top.

Beyond the arch, Juliet saw the sloping lawn of the house grounds and a blue corner of the big pool. Kemo, Cody's dog, stood between the pillars, wagging his tail in a hopeful manner. Juliet waved at the mutt and caught a brief glimpse of the rambling two-story house before they sped past and turned into the small drive that led to the guesthouse next door.

Juliet finished her tale as he pulled up before the little house she rented from him.

"So that's that," she told him. "I'm making myself a whole new kind of life, from now on."

He gave her his beautiful right-sided smile. "And then what happens?"

"When?"

"After Midsummer Madness is over. After you've proved beyond a doubt that you're the most assertive woman around."

"Well," she confessed, "I haven't thought that far ahead yet." She scooped up her jacket and her manila folder and leaned on the door latch. It gave, and she jumped down. "But I'll let you know, as soon as I figure it out. If you're still interested, that is."

She turned and practically skipped up the stone walk to the small porch of the guesthouse before she realized that in her excitement over all she'd accomplished, she'd forgotten to thank Cody for the lift home.

Conveniently, he hadn't driven away yet but was still sitting there staring after her, with his engine idling. She rushed back to the driver's side and leaned in the window.

"Thanks, Cody. Thanks a bunch." She kissed his cheek— it was warm and a little rough, very pleasant to the lips, actually. And then she whirled and danced back up the walk.

Cody sat and watched her go, bewildered at the change in her. Why, damned if her blouse hadn't been open two buttons down. He'd got himself the sweetest glimpse of that little shadow between her small, high breasts when she leaned in the window and put her soft lips on his cheek.

He couldn't figure it. What in the hell was innocent Julie Huddleston doing showing cleavage, making a man think about her in a whole new way?

He had half a mind to call her back and tell her to button up. But she was already bouncing up the steps of the guesthouse, turning once to wave, and disappearing inside.

Cody sat there a few minutes more, deciding that telling her to button up would have been presumptuous anyway. He was glad he hadn't done it. It would have sounded nothing short of crude—and besides, then she would have known that Cody McIntyre, who had always looked *out* for her, had just now been looking *down* her blouse.

Three

––––

Juliet's only problem that night was getting to sleep. She was just too keyed up to simply close her eyes and drift off. So she lay with the window open and only a sheet for a cover, staring up at the ceiling and enjoying daydreams of her success.

She planned a little, thinking it would be fun to try to get a real professional auctioneer this year to raffle off the baked goods at the big picnic on closing day. And this year, for the frog jump, she was going to see that there were separate categories for out-of-county frogs. Recently, some tourists had been buying some real long jumpers from Sacramento pet stores and running them against the more short-hocked local frogs. It just wasn't fair.

Smiling into the darkness, Juliet rolled over and tried to settle down. But ideas kept coming. She thought of a better way to arrange the booth spaces for the Crafts and Industry Fair even as she started planning her own costume for the

Gold Rush Ball. Maybe she'd go as Maria Elena Roderica Perez Smith, the doomed laundress from local history. Or as one-eyed Charlie Parkhurst, who'd lived her life pretending to be a man. Or maybe Madame Moustache, the lusty bighearted saloon owner of Nevada City fame....

Juliet rolled over again and looked at the clock; it was past midnight. She really ought to get some sleep. Tomorrow was Friday, a regular workday. She had to finish off the payrolls for Duane's Coffee Shop and Babe Allen's Gift and Card Emporium, not to mention get a good start on that unit cost analysis for McMulch's Lumberyard.

From outside, she heard the crow of a rooster who was up way past his bedtime. Juliet grinned. She knew the rooster. The ranch, which was mostly timberland, didn't support too many animals. Cody kept three horses, Kemo the dog and a cow called Emeline. There were a few chickens pecking around the stables, and one big mean black rooster that Cody swore was destined to be thrown in the pot one day soon. Cody called him Black Bart, and he was the only one ornery enough to stay up making noise all night.

Black Bart crowed again. And as the sound of his crowing faded off into the night, Juliet heard, drifting in the open window, the sweet, high sound of a harmonica.

It was Cody. Playing that silver mouth organ of his in the way that only he knew how, the notes sliding all over the scale, from so high and sweet your heart ached, to those low, sexy notes that vibrated down inside a person in the most stimulating way. Lord, Juliet thought, that boy could make music. No wonder his songs drove the ladies wild.

For a while she just lay there, as she had many a night since she took the guesthouse, her senses gratified and her spirit soothed by the impromptu concert that drifted through the window on the night air.

And then it occurred to her that getting Cody to perform in the Midsummer Madness Revue would be a coup of sorts. Every year they asked him, and every year he very courteously declined. Cody would provide goods and capital to the festival, but he always claimed he was too busy to commit himself to getting up on the stage every single night.

Juliet closed her eyes and hummed along a little, until her own lack of musical talent made her fall silent, so that she could better enjoy the magic spell that Cody could weave with just a song.

Yes, she thought, as he began a new tune, she would definitely ask him. As she'd learned in assertiveness training, nothing was ever lost by asking. If the answer was no, you were in no worse a position than before you asked; if you got a yes, you were one ahead. Besides, maybe Cody would agree to perform if Juliet was the one asking. Maybe he'd do it for the sake of their lifelong friendship—if she caught him in the right mood.

As the second tune ended on a high note, the thought came to her: Why not just go ask him now?

She nodded at the ceiling. Yes, that would be a good approach. To ask him right now, spontaneously, in the middle of the night when neither of them seemed to be able to sleep.

Juliet pushed back the sheet and rose from her bed. She pulled on her light robe over her pajamas and decided not to even worry about her feet. She could use the little iron gate in the stone fence between the two houses. That way, there were only smooth paving stones and soft grass between his house and hers.

She went out the back door and down the few steps to the stone walk that led to the gate. The stones, as she padded from one to the next, were still warm from a summer day's worth of sun.

Overhead there was no moon, but the stars were very bright. The gold grasses of the open pasture on her right, which was separated from her house by a wooden fence, seemed to reflect the starlight, so Juliet had no trouble seeing the way. She flew past the hay barn and small stables, which loomed just on the other side of the fence. Cody began another song as she pulled open the gate to the main grounds and slipped through.

Beyond the gate was another world. Six acres of sloping, manicured grass were bisected by a gravel drive that ended in a roomy garage. On the near side of the drive lay the swimming pool, lit now and casting its eerie light up toward the night sky. On the far side of the drive, up a walk lined with rose bushes, was the house, a two-story white clapboard structure with green roof and trim.

Originally, as Cody's mother had once explained to Juliet, the guesthouse had been the main house. The ranch had been smaller then, more of a homestead than anything else. Cody's great-grandmother had run the place, while his great-grandfather owned and operated the Rush Creek Digs mine. They'd closed the mine in Cody's grandfather's time; Cody's grandfather had bought more land, then built his family a bigger, more comfortable place to live. Cody's father, retired and living in Arizona for the past few years, had opened the hardware store in town and added the Olympic-size pool at the house. When he retired, Cody's dad had signed both the ranch and hardware store over to his only son. Now Cody took care of it all, as well as the bar and grill that was his contribution to the family holdings.

The huge yard of the main house was surrounded on three sides by a stone wall. The north side, except for the garage, was divided from the pasture by a wooden fence. It was a stunning effect, Juliet had always thought: the pampered, lush grounds, cut off from the road and the outbuildings by the high wall—but opened right up to the wild, wide field on the north side. There, the tall grasses rolled away for a half mile or so until they hit the woodlands of the surrounding hills.

Once inside the gate and sheltered by the spreading shadow of a big fruitless mulberry tree there, Juliet hesitated, partly in hushed appreciation of the starlit yard, and partly to gauge the source of the music that curled through the still night.

The melody came, as she had suspected, from the wide front porch that faced her across the drive. She could see Cody there, now that she looked for him. Since the porch light was off, he sat in shadow, lounging against one of the two pillars that flanked the front steps. He faced the main gate and had his back to the garage. He was shirtless—she could see the sheen of bare skin—and barefoot, too, just as she was. His naked feet were on the second step. Not far away from him, near the porch railing, she could make out the sprawled black shape of the dog, Kemo. The dog's head was raised and pointed in her direction.

Cody, staring off toward the front gate, seemed lost in his music. If he had looked, he could have seen her, even in the shadow of the mulberry, for her robe was the palest shade of blue and drew what little light there was within the darkness. But he didn't look.

Kemo, still peering in Juliet's direction, whined. Cody stopped playing to murmur a soft order to the animal. The dog laid his sleek black head on his paws once more.

Juliet stood for a while, listening to the song, suspended in the moment and glad to be there. All of her senses seemed heightened. There was the music, the faint gleam of Cody's skin across the yard, the cool caress of moist grass at her feet. The grass had a sweet, full earthy smell that mingled deliciously with the dusty scent of the drier, wilder grass on the other side of the fence.

Cody paused for a breath. From somewhere on the green lawn, a frog croaked; it was a rough, humorous sound, after the beguiling beauty of the song. Juliet smiled. Cody played on.

It occurred to her that, were she to circle the pool and cross the drive up by the garage, she could approach from the side steps and keep from disturbing Cody for a few minutes more. It seemed appropriate, somehow, for her to come up on him quietly. It was in keeping with the enchanted mood of moonless darkness and haunting song.

The thick grass tickled her feet as she crept, still smiling to herself, beneath the trees that grew close to the stone wall. By the time she reached the wooden fence, it had become a sort of game to her. She shot across the open space, picked her way over the pebbles of the drive in front of the garage and then flew across the unprotected space on the other side. Then she had one of the pair of huge old chestnut trees that grew in front of the house for cover as she approached the side of the porch.

When she put her dew-damp foot on the bottom step, Cody began yet another song, one of his own that Juliet had heard once or twice over the years. It was a love song, about a poor boy who loved a rich girl whose family kept them apart. Now, of course, he only played the melody. But Juliet recalled the general flow of the lyrics, and felt sad for the penniless lover, whose dream girl could never be his.

Juliet mounted the steps and then, still unchallenged, began to approach the man who sat on the front steps with his back to her, playing one of those songs that broke women's hearts.

The wooden boards of the porch were with her; they gave out nary a squeak. The dog, too, seemed to be on her side.

Though he raised his head and watched her, he made no sound.

Juliet tiptoed to the Mission-style easy chair, one of a pair that flanked the double front door. And then, lost in the music, she hovered there, staring at the marvelously sculpted musculature of Cody's bare back, until the sad song came to an end.

There was a silence, one that slowly filled up with the sounds of the night. An owl hooted somewhere behind the house. The crickets spun out whirring songs of their own. A mourning dove cried. Out in the field, a quail loosed its piping call, just as Kemo's snaky black tail began beating the porch boards, and the dog opened his mouth to pant in a welcoming way.

Cody said, "Julie."

He said it softly, in a different way than anyone had ever said her name before. He turned his head, slowly, and smiled at her.

Juliet smiled back, with no shyness or hesitation. It seemed that her triumph at the meeting earlier had boosted her confidence, while the magic safety of the darkness made her bold.

"You saw me," she accused in a teasing manner, as Kemo rose and went to her to be scratched behind the ear.

Cody nodded. "When you came through the gate."

"The music was so beautiful. I didn't want to break the mood. So I sneaked up on you, hoping that you wouldn't stop." The dog, satisfactorily scratched, went to the end of the porch nearest the front gate. There, he walked in a circle, at last lying down again, all curled into himself.

Juliet came to sit next to Cody, first adjusting her robe where it met on her lap, then wrapping her hands around her knees. "I've enjoyed it each time you played, ever since I moved in."

"You never came over before. How come?"

She glanced off toward the rippling lights of the pool. "I don't know. I guess I was just never the kind of woman to run across a lawn barefoot in the middle of the night."

"But now you are?"

Juliet chuckled, considering the question, considering her own lightness of spirit, her boldness, her sense of glowing self-confidence. Tonight, she felt disconnected from her usual self. It was as if her usual self were some other woman, a woman for whom she felt a little sorry. A woman frightened of life, of its sights, scents and sounds, of its sweet and sensual beauty that tonight seemed created for her alone.

"Well?"

"What?" She looked at him.

"I asked if now you were the kind of woman who—"

"I remember. And I don't know. Tonight is different. I feel different. But we'll see."

He smiled again, that slow warm smile that lifted the right side of his mouth a fraction more than the left. Juliet thought, as he did that, that it was fully understandable why the women went wild for him.

Lord, he was one beautiful hunk of man. Much too much man for someone like Juliet—she knew that. But absolutely splendid nonetheless.

"Believe it or not," she went on, in an effort to distract herself from the surplus of masculine splendor before her— from the hard, broad chest, the corded neck, the gleaming eyes and the right-sided smile, "I did come over here with a specific purpose in mind."

"And that was?"

"To ask you a favor."

He was watching her mouth. "A favor?" He repeated the word right after her, as if he'd caught it from her lips and then playfully tossed it back her way.

"Yes," she confirmed, surprised at the steadiness of her own voice. Inside, she was drowning in the most wonderful yearning sort of feeling, an utterly delicious feeling, one she was sure she should restrain, but one to which she wanted to give free rein.

"Well?"

She recollected her supposed purposed. "It's about the revue."

"The Midsummer Madness Revue?"

"Yes."

"What about it?"

"Well, I was thinking..."

"Yeah?"

"I was *hoping,* actually...."

"You were thinking and hoping what?"

She went ahead and said it right out at last. "I would really appreciate it if you would agree to sing a song or two in the revue this year."

He said nothing for a moment. Then he murmured her name in a regretful tone, and she knew that next he'd be telling her how busy he was.

In a gesture that seemed perfectly natural, she put a finger on his lips. "Shh. Don't answer now. Just think about it. Okay?"

"I don't think so," he told her. His lips were firm, his breath warm on her skin. It was a lovely sensation, touching his mouth, feeling the movement beneath her fingers each time he spoke.

Juliet shook herself, remembering that, no matter how good his lips felt, they were getting dangerously close to saying "no" to her request. She shushed him again. "Didn't I ask you not to answer now?"

He smiled, which she felt as a brushing softness on the pads of her fingers. "All right. I'll think about it."

"Good." She gave a satisfied little nod, and then realized she couldn't go on touching his lips forever, no matter how good it felt. She pulled her hand away and faced the pool again. He didn't move. She could feel his eyes on her.

A little silence happened, one that had a peculiar edge to it. A precipitous edge, Juliet thought.

She turned to him. "I, um, suppose I should go back to my house now."

"Why?" He seemed to be looking at her mouth. And then her neck, and the little V that was formed where her pajamas buttoned up and the facings of her robe met.

"Well, I . . . I did what I came out here to do. I asked you to be in the revue."

"That's all you came out here for? To ask me to be in the revue?"

She nodded.

He didn't seem to believe that. "You sure?"

When she'd touched his mouth to hush him, she'd scooted right up next to him. And then, even when she'd looked off at the pool, she hadn't actually moved away. So now she was seeing him at very close range.

It was an enthralling experience. So near, his male beauty was absolutely mesmerizing. She stared at him, forgetting to even try to talk, marveling at the perfection of his firm mouth, his symmetrical nose, his shiny brown hair.

Goodness—the realization caused her to hitch in a quick breath—why, she wanted to kiss him! Her lips were practically twitching with the longing to be pressed to his.

He looked back at her, and it was as if he *knew* her forbidden wish, because the impossible happened. He shifted forward just a fraction and her wish came true.

They were kissing.

It couldn't be happening—but it was.

And it felt wonderful. He made a lovely, rough sound in his throat, and his hard, naked arms went around her. She heard the harmonica clatter on the porch boards as he pulled her up against him.

Ah, how utterly delightful. Juliet didn't want to pull away. So she didn't.

His hands rubbed her back in slow, sweet circles, and his lips played with hers for a while, teasing and nibbling, kind of getting to know her mouth.

And then his tongue got involved, slipping out to press at the little seam between her lips. Juliet gasped at first, since she'd never in her life been familiar with another person's tongue. But then she felt herself go easy and soft in his arms, because being familiar with Cody's tongue felt just fine. Just terrific, after all.

Since his tongue seemed to hint at the possibility that she might allow her lips to part, she did it, with a little sigh.

He whispered "Julie," and then his tongue slipped in. She smiled in welcome, liking it immensely, and even shyly touching the gentle intruder with her own tongue. The deepened kiss continued.

And then he pulled away. She gave a cry. But the loss of such joy was only temporary. He only wanted, she learned soon enough, to do a little rearranging of their bodies before he kissed her some more.

He turned her and guided her down, across his lap, cradling her on one arm, so he could sip from her mouth some more.

Juliet raised her lips eagerly to him, and stroked his shoulders, deeply pleasured by the taut feel of his skin, and the hard bulge of the muscles beneath.

"Oh, Cody." She sighed against his mouth. "Oh, Cody, how wonderful.... No one ever told me..."

He chuckled at that, a husky chuckle that seemed to ignite all her senses the more. She went on stroking his sleek shoulders, and then sliding her fingers up to toy in the silky hair at his nape.

Meanwhile, he was not idle. Besides the long, drugging kiss that never seemed to end, his free hand caressed her, in long strokes at first. From the slim curve of her hip, to the cove of her waist, it moved up to slide along her rib cage, then back down again.

Somehow, the belt of her robe was gone, the robe fully parted. Cody's exploring hand drifted over her hip, bringing the hem of her pajama top along, until he was rubbing the bare skin of her waist beneath the top.

Oh, it was heaven. How on earth could she have lived for thirty whole years and known next to nothing of this heady bliss? It was better than anything. Better than ice cream on a sweltering day, better than hot cocoa of a cold winter's night. Better than— Oh, Lord, yes, it was true—better than driving her red car, or running Midsummer Madness for the first time in her life!

This *was* Midsummer Madness. Incredible. Divine.

Cody's warm, big hand slid up her waist—and, light as a breath, skimmed the nipple of her left breast.

"Oh, my goodness!" Juliet gasped.

His hand repeated the action. Juliet gasped again. And then—

He pulled away.

Juliet, who realized her eyes were dreamily closed, opened them. She looked into Cody's eyes, which were heavy-lidded and full of sensual promise. "I said, 'oh, my goodness,'" she pointed out. "I didn't say stop."

Juliet found she didn't regret her bold words when, for a moment, it looked as if he might resume where he'd left off—lower his mouth to where she could get at it, and start doing those lovely things with his hand again.

But the moment stretched out too long, and she had to admit that his expression had rearranged itself; he was now looking more stern than aroused.

Gently he guided her to a sitting position once more and handed her the belt to her robe, which had somehow ended up wrapped around his neck.

He said, "I shouldn't have done that."

Juliet, attempting to take things in stride, decided to be grateful for what she got. "I know," she replied, "but I surely do thank you anyway, Cody McIntyre."

Cody frowned at that. "Don't thank me," he said, rather harshly, she thought.

"But I—"

He cut her off. "Let it go." Then he relented a little. "I went too far. I'm sorry."

"You did?" She thought about that. "I don't know. Isn't . . . what you did natural? I didn't ask you to stop."

"Damn it, Julie. You're a virgin."

Juliet's face flamed at the blunt way he said that. She turned away.

"Well, aren't you?" he demanded.

She couldn't bring herself to look at him, but she managed to nod.

He swore again. "That's what I mean. You don't know what the hell you're doing. And damn it, neither do I. I don't take advantage of virgins."

Juliet wished she could crawl under the porch. Her ears were on fire from hearing Cody talk so bluntly about her lack of experience. She almost lurched to her feet and ran across the lawn for home. But then she decided that one of the reasons she was still a virgin at thirty was a distinct lack of nerve. She'd never really get to experience life if she always backed down. So she forced herself to stay put and dared to speak. "Well, um, then," she began somewhat wiltingly. She drew in a bracing breath and went on with more gumption, "If you don't take advantage of virgins, then why did you kiss me?"

He granted her another long look. Then he muttered with feeling, "Hell, Julie...."

She stared right back at him. "'Hell, Julie,' is not an answer."

"Damn it...."

"Neither is 'damn it.'"

"Look, I didn't mean it to go so far—I didn't mean it to go *anywhere.*"

Juliet felt a sad little sinking feeling in her heart when he said that, but she went ahead with her next question anyway. "Well, what did you mean, then?"

"I don't know," he said, finger-combing his hair and shifting on the step. "I couldn't sleep. I came out here to play myself a lullaby. And then you came, trying to sneak up on me. It was like a game, and I started playing. I wanted to kiss you, so I did kiss you. And it went further than it should have."

Juliet, absorbed in her own confusions, didn't fully realize what a rough time Cody was having. He was both frustrated in his desire, *and* disgusted at himself for toying with an innocent. Partly in an effort to get his bearings—and also in an attempt to hide the evidence that his lust still wasn't exactly under control—Cody slid even farther away from her on the step until he was practically wrapped around the big post that supported the porch roof.

Juliet noted his withdrawal, and thought regretfully of the delicious caress of his hand on her breast—a caress she was becoming more and more certain she would never experience again. She forced herself to take a long, hard look at the situation—and to recall that a man like Cody McIntyre was not a man for her.

She said, a little sadly but very firmly, "You're right." She solemnly nodded. "We went too far."

Cody listened with only half his attention; he was still pondering the prospect of trying to stand up without embarrassing himself.

Juliet rebelted her robe and tied it with a no-nonsense tug. "We'll just have to forget this ever happened, okay?" She rearranged the robe to cover her knees. "A gorgeous man like you is nothing but trouble for a plain woman like me."

Forgetting the problem with his jeans, Cody whipped his head around to face her again, ready to inform her that looks do not make the man—and to add, for her information, that he didn't find her plain at all. Lately.

But she prattled on before he could get a word in. "You've been good to me over the years. You always stood up for me when Billy Butley used to pick on me back in school, and you were my first client when I opened my service. I'll always like you. A lot. But I don't want to get mixed up with you. I'd only get my heart broken, and that's a simple fact."

"Now wait a minute—"

"No. You wait. Cody, the women are always after you. And one of these days, one of them would be sure to tempt you right away from me."

Cody stared at her. He had half a mind to point out to her just how wrong she was. He could use his father as an example. From the time he met Cody's mother, Wayne McIntyre had never so much as *looked* at another woman. Cody's grandfather, Yancy, had been the same way. Cody came from a long line of truehearted men. No other woman could tempt him away from the woman he'd chosen for his own....

But then again, telling her that might give her the wrong idea. After all, he'd only just kissed her for the first time a few minutes ago. And though he'd like to do a hell of a lot more than kiss her, he had no intention of getting into anything permanent—not on such short notice, anyway.

Besides, as he'd been doing his damndest to explain to her, only a jerk would seek a casual affair with an innocent like Juliet. Cody always did his best not to behave like a jerk.

But then, *was* this casual? It didn't exactly feel casual. Something *had* happened to him. Her innocence, coupled with this bewitching new frankness, had him spinning. He didn't know which way was up.

She was so different than the women he'd known—women who understood completely what they were getting into when they made love with a man. However, it was true that the past few years, he'd been spending more and more nights alone. The experienced ladies who always seemed to seek him out just didn't do much for him anymore—though he hadn't given a lot of thought to what he might be looking for instead.

Could Julie be it?

The question bounced around his brain like an echo in a mine shaft. It was a damn dangerous question, and one he wasn't prepared to answer tonight. It would be insane to try to.

That's why he had to do something—very soon. Because if he sat there any longer looking at her in her pajamas and thin robe and remembering the feel of her mouth under his, he damn well might just go ahead and decide that Julie Huddleston—who'd been here all along—was the woman he'd been waiting thirty years to find.

He'd end up acting like a man who'd gone over the edge completely. He'd be begging her on bended knee to give him one chance—or promising that he'd never so much as look at another woman for the rest of their lives!

Cody stood up, wincing a little when his jeans bound that part of him that refused to take orders from his brain. "Whatever you want," he croaked. "It's fine with me."

Juliet swallowed, looking up at him, wishing she could grab his leg and trip him ... so that he fell into her waiting arms. Lord, he was beautiful.

But not the man for her.

"I'm glad you understand," she said.

He bent to scoop up the harmonica and then turned for the door.

"Um, Cody?"

"What?" He half turned back to her.

"Just forget what I asked you, about being in the revue, okay? We're around each other a lot anyway. Might as well not make it worse."

"Sure. Fine," he said. "Kemo." The dog lifted his head and thumped his tail. "Come on." Kemo rose and followed his master inside.

Juliet felt bereft when the door closed and left her on the front porch alone. Cody had been so curt and abrupt. He'd never behaved that way toward her.

But, then, he'd never kissed her and touched her breast before, either.

Juliet stood up and pulled her robe closer about her. Then she began the short stroll back to her own little house.

When she climbed into bed again and settled under the sheet, she told herself that it would all work out fine in the end. She and Cody had been friends for too long for one foolish indiscretion to make all that much difference in how they behaved toward each other.

She'd stay away from him for a few days, and then things would settle back into their normal routine. In a week or two, everything would be just as it had always been between them. She was sure of it.

Four

———

WANTED

Singers. Actors. Dancers. Performers of all types and persuasions. Get involved. Help the community. Try out this year for the MIDSUMMER MADNESS REVUE. Town Auditorium, 401 Broad Street. Monday, July 15, 7–10 p.m. For more information call 555-3462.

Cody tried to ignore the notice as he walked past it. It was posted in the window of his restaurant, right beside the copy of the open menu. It had been there for four days—since Friday, when Flat-nosed Jake had strolled in with a stack of the things and asked to be allowed to put one up where it would be seen by everyone.

Cody had told him to go ahead and stick it in the front window. It hadn't even occurred to Cody that, over the next few days, he might find it bothersome, to see it out of the corner of his eye every time he went in the front door.

In previous years, the revue had never been anything more than something he enjoyed as a member of the audience—and tactfully avoided as a potential performer. But for some reason, this year, he couldn't get the thing out of his mind. He blamed this preoccupation on the damn notice, which he had to walk by umpteen times a day. The fact that Julie was directing the revue, and had ended up asking him *not* to get involved, had nothing to do with his irritation. Julie's request that he stay out of it fell right in with his own intentions. He didn't want to get involved—never had, never would. If it wasn't for that notice, he wouldn't even have to *think* about getting involved.

In fact, thinking about it, he realized he could choose *not* to think about it. And that was exactly what he intended to do.

Having decided never again to notice the notice, Cody strode grimly into the cool, dim interior of McIntyre's. To his left, the long mahogany bar gleamed. Around the divider that sectioned off the main restaurant, he caught a glimpse of one of the tables, set for four. The polished wooden surface of the table looked comfortable and inviting. The glassware sparkled in the recessed overhead light. At the reservation podium, his night hostess was greeting a party of six and turning to lead them to their seats.

Cody made for the bar. He sat at the end, where there were some vacant stools, and signaled to one of the bartenders for a draft beer. The bartender, as per instructions, served Cody only when all the customers were content.

When the beer was set before him, Cody asked, "Where's Archie?" There were two bartenders behind the counter; one of them at this hour on Monday night should have been Archie Kent.

"I traded shifts with him, just for tonight," the substitute, Bob Meeker, quickly explained.

"Everything okay with him? Is he sick?" Cody asked.

"Oh yeah, he's fine. He wants to check out the revue—see if he can get involved."

"What for?"

"You know Archie. A big ham."

"A big ham with a *job*," Cody trenchantly pointed out.

Bob Meeker shrugged. "He's on days now, remember? That is, except for Monday nights. He figured he could work it out, if he got a part. He's pretty excited about it, if you want to know the truth—ever since the bookkeeper got a hold of him."

"What bookkeeper?"

"You know. *Your* bookkeeper. Ms. Huddleston."

"Julie." Cody muttered the name with bleak resignation. Then, suspiciously, "What do you mean '*got a hold* of him'?"

"You know, since she worked on him to try out."

"Was she in here?"

"Yes."

Something tightened inside of Cody. He felt disappointed and hurt. He'd hardly seen Julie since last Thursday night when he'd gone out on the porch to relax himself with music and ended up with her in his arms. She'd been avoiding him since then—he knew it. It was understandable that she'd want a little distance between them after what had happened. So her avoiding him probably shouldn't bother him. But it did.

"When was she in here?"

"Saturday. During the break after lunch."

"When I wasn't." Cody muttered the words more to himself than to Bob.

"Er, right. She passed out flyers, said she was making the rounds of all the businesses on Broad and over on Commercial, too. She said she was reminding everyone about the revue and that they were welcome to come out for it." Bob Meeker gave a musing chuckle. "Took us all by surprise at first, her speaking up like that, strolling up to each of us, smiling a big how-do-you-do and then launching into her little pitch. She didn't hardly seem like the same scared little mouse who's been creeping around here, scared of her own shadow, for as long as any of us can remember."

Cody growled, "What do you mean, 'creeping'? Julie never creeped—er, crept."

Bob Meeker, who wanted to keep his job, agreed, "Whatever you say, Cody."

"Tell me what happened between her and Archie." The command came out a little harsher than Cody might have intended.

Bob Meeker looked at him sideways. "You okay, boss?"

"I'm fine. Tell me."

"Nothing happened. She could see he was interested, so she talked to him a little longer than she did the rest of us."

"How much longer?"

"Look, Cody, it really wasn't a big deal."

"Fine. Just tell me."

"I don't know." Bob polished the bar. "A few minutes, maybe. She said how glad they'd be if he could take a part in one of the little plays they're doing, or something like that."

Cody pictured Archie in his mind—sandy-colored hair and a ready smile, good-looking and personable. Women liked Archie. He was charming and boyish. Maybe too charming—not for a bartender, of course, but too charming by a long shot for Julie.

Someone like Archie Kent wouldn't be right for Julie at all. Julie was innocent, damn it. She had to be careful of charming men who would not take her seriously. Hell, if Cody was willing to put his own desires aside and protect her from *himself*, he couldn't go letting someone like Archie Kent take advantage of her, now could he?

Bob Meeker, who knew a chance to escape when he saw one, had moved to the center of the bar and begun studiously washing glasses, shoving them on the scrubber-covered posts in the frothy dishwater, scooping them through the rinse and setting them to drain. Still, he had enough curiosity in him to inquire as Cody made for the door, "Where you going, boss?"

He got no answer. Cody was already gone.

"Unhand me this very instant, *señor!* I am a married woman. My husband will not like what you do!"

"Gimme a kiss...."

"No!"

"Yes!"

"Oh! I warn you, *señor!*"

"Stop fighting me, sweet thing...."

"No, no, I will not have my honor besmirched ... I warn you...."

"Ha-ha. You little wildcat.... Argh, ah! My God, you've stabbed me, you scurrilous wench!"

"Okay, that was wonderful. You can stop now," Juliet said.

The couple up on the stage lowered the looseleaf notebooks they were reading from and looked expectantly down at Juliet in the front row.

"Give us just a minute," Juliet told the two, then she went back several rows to confer with Melda Cooks, the author of the piece, which was entitled, *The Mysterious and Sus-*

*picious Events Surrounding the Cruel and Untimely Death
by Hanging of Maria Elena Roderica Perez Smith.*

"What do you think?" Juliet kept her voice low.

"They're splendid." Melda peered over the top edge of
her thick spectacles. "I was enthralled."

"So we have our laundress and the man she stabbed."

"As far as I'm concerned, we do."

Juliet was pleased. She'd especially encouraged Archie
Kent, the man up on the stage, to come to tryouts. And the
woman, Yolanda Hughes, was just perfect for the part of
Maria Elena, who killed a man and hung for it rather than
lose her honor. It was said that Maria Elena had possessed
"shining black eyes and a lush mane of hair to match." Yolanda, who owned and operated a hairdressing salon, fit the
bill physically and had some acting talent as well.

Juliet went back to the couple on the stage, thanked them
and told them to be sure to leave phone numbers with Andrea Oakleaf, who was acting as her assistant tonight. Then
she turned to the small group of people in the first rows who
still hadn't had a chance to get up on the stage and read
something.

"Now," she told them, "how about if you three—" she
gestured at two men and a woman who were sitting together "—open up to page 22, which is a scene from the
Living History Play...." She went on to tell them which
parts to read and was just waiting for them to move onto the
stage, when the big double doors at the head of the center
aisle were pulled back. She glanced up.

It was Cody, whom she'd not only been avoiding, but
whom she'd been trying her best not to think about, since
Thursday night. At the sight of him, her pulse was suddenly racing, and her cheeks felt pink.

She could think of no reason why the sight of a man she'd
known all her life should suddenly send her senses into

overload. But somehow, in the past few days, he had suddenly become even better looking than before—which surely wasn't possible. Was it? She stared at him in his dark slacks and Western shirt and tooled boots that he wore evenings at his restaurant and wondered: had his chest always been so broad and deep, his hips so marvelously lean and hard?

Yolanda Hughes, who was gathering up her huge purse from a seat near where Juliet stood, murmured dreamily, "God, what a hunk...." Then, realizing that Juliet had heard, she gave a husky laugh. "I can't help it, the man is pure eye candy."

Juliet felt her irritation rise—and for the purest of motives, she told herself. All these years, women had been fighting being made into objects, and here was a woman doing the same thing to a man. "He's much more than that," she shot back, only aware after the words were out how self-righteous—and self-incriminating—they would sound.

Yolanda, swinging her bag over her shoulder, muttered, "Some girls have all the luck..." as she sauntered toward the side door.

In the meantime, Andrea Oakleaf saw an opportunity to improve the revue—and took it. She jumped out of her seat and marched up to Cody, a triumphant gleam in her gunmetal-gray eyes. "Cody McIntyre!" She gave a nod, and the tight bun on the back of her head bounced briskly. "How heartening. It's about time you decided to donate your talents to the revue."

Cody, who'd entered looking extremely purposeful, suddenly hesitated and backed up a step. "Now, Miss Oakleaf, let's not go jumping to conclusions. I didn't come here with trying out in mind."

Juliet jumped in to help him out. "Yes, Andrea. Cody's much too busy—"

"Pshaw," said Miss Oakleaf, who knew way too much about most folks in Emerald Gap, since she'd once been just about everyone's kindergarten teacher. "He's a spoiled only child who thinks it will kill him to make a commitment of his time for a few hours a night a few days in the summer."

"Aw, come on Miss Oakleaf." Cody sounded a little hurt. "Is that fair?"

Andrea thought about that. "Well, all right. Perhaps the word *spoiled* is too strong. But it's still about time you gave us a song or two in the revue."

"That's the truth, and you know it, Cody." Flat-nosed Jake spoke up from over near the stage.

"Yeah, get involved, Cody!" one of the auditioners said.

Someone else chimed in, "Sing us a song. We need you!"

"Come on, Cody!"

"Where's your community spirit?"

Cody looked as trapped as he probably felt. Juliet stared at him, wondering what could have brought him here. Before, he'd always had the sense to be nowhere in sight when revue auditions were in progress. He was shaking his head, making sorry-but-I-really-can't noises, when Archie Kent, who had disappeared toward the rest rooms for a moment and just now returned, piped up with "Yeah, boss. Help us out a little, will you?"

Cody stopped looking sheepish so suddenly it was almost comical and turned a hard glare on Archie. "*You're* the one I'm looking for."

Archie's easy smile fled. "Hey, what's the matter? Didn't Bob show up? He promised to fill in for me...."

"Bob showed up," Cody answered stiffly.

Archie was now looking somewhat bewildered. "Then what's the problem?"

"The problem is..." Cody's voice trailed off. It was as if he himself didn't know what the problem was.

"Yeah?" Archie prompted.

"The problem is....you don't have time for this, that's what. You know how busy we get during the festival."

"But, Cody. I'm on *days*." Poor Archie now looked utterly confused.

And Juliet didn't blame him. Cody had always been generous with his people when it came to the festival. All the merchants in town were, because the festival brought in droves of tourists; tourists were the major industry of Emerald Gap. In fact, many businesses counted on bringing in up to twenty percent of their yearly income during the ten days of Midsummer Madness. For Cody to keep any one of his employees from the revue—especially when there was no serious scheduling conflict—made no sense at all.

Juliet's own bafflement was clear in her voice when she asked, "Cody, what has come over you?" She reached for poor Archie's arm and patted it reassuringly. "*I* talked Archie into trying out. I was sure you wouldn't mind. You never have before."

Cody didn't look her in the face. He seemed to be glaring at her hand, where it lay on Archie's arm. "Well, this time is different," he growled.

"But how?" She gave Archie's arm one more pat and then dropped her hand.

At last Cody looked into her eyes. She felt a hot little shiver, something quick and alive, arrowing down into the center of her, and spreading outward, like the ripples in a pond.

"It's different," Cody said, scowling. "And I want a few words alone with you, Juliet, to explain just how."

Juliet. He'd called her Juliet. Not in all the memory of their friendship had he called her by her full name, or addressed her in such a stiff, cold manner.

Juliet's heart sank. He'd been curt and gruff with her on Thursday night, but she'd understood that, given what had happened. She'd been sure in a few days everything would be fine between them again. However, looking at him now, she could see things were not fine. What in the world could she have done to have made him so angry with her?

It hurt in the worst way, to have him look at her with such disdain—and in front of all these people, too. The auditorium seemed suddenly very quiet. Juliet realized that she and Cody were the focus of everyone's attention. They were all watching, wondering what would happen next.

At that moment, all of her former shyness chose to flood back in on her. The ultimate nightmare of her timorous self was happening. Everyone was looking at her, speculating about what was actually going on here between plain Juliet Huddleston and gorgeous Cody McIntyre, every woman's dream.

Juliet longed to just open her mouth and tell Cody that to talk alone would be fine. But for the moment, she was paralyzed with timidity. She managed, somehow, to glance at Jake, who had come nearer during the last exchange and now stood by her right shoulder. Since Thursday night, she'd talked with Jake several times, discussing the flyers, and the newspaper notice, and how he and Andrea would help her run the tryouts. Now, after spending all of her life thinking of Flat-nosed Jake as that old eccentric who lived in the log house way out in the woods, she also had started to think of him as her friend. She telegraphed him a pleading look.

Jake seemed to hear her wordless call for help. He grinned and broke the awful silence. "Good idea, Cody. You two wrangle it out later. Now, we got these auditions to finish up."

"Yes, everyone's waiting," Andrea Oakleaf concurred. Then she added with a crafty smile, "You just agree to sing us two songs, young man, and you may be excused."

Cody, who had been staring way too hard at Juliet, managed to drag his gaze away to try to stand up to his kindergarten teacher. "Now, wait a minute—"

"No, *you* wait, Cody McIntyre," Miss Oakleaf snapped back. "You finagled your way out of directing the whole festival this year, and our Juliet here is doing your job for you. The least you can do in return is perform in the revue. I want a commitment, young man."

"But—"

"A commitment."

Cody finger-combed his hair. "Hell."

"Two songs."

There was another of those hanging silences. Then Cody finally gave in. "All right. I'll do it."

There was actually a smattering of applause. "Good going, boss!" Archie cheered.

Cody gave his employee a look that had him waving goodbye and out of there within seconds. Then Cody turned his eyes on Juliet. "Is your car fixed yet?"

She somehow found her voice. "Uh, no. They, um, told me tomorrow for sure." She was still using his spare pickup truck.

"Fine. You can drive me home, and we'll talk then. I'll be at the restaurant, as soon as you're through here."

"O-okay," she stammered.

He curtly nodded and turned for the big doors at the top of the aisle. Juliet watched him go, thinking that this thing with Cody simply was not turning out as she'd thought it would.

Staying out of his way for a few days, until things got back to normal between them, didn't seem to have done one bit of good. Not when he could march in here and, with no more than a look, make her insides turn to molten lava. Not when he now seemed angrier with her than he had been when he left her on the porch the other night. Not when he was suddenly behaving completely unlike himself, demanding that poor Archie not take part in the revue.

"Juliet?" Andrea asked. "Shall we resume where we left off?"

Juliet valiantly put her worries about Cody away until the proper time to deal with them. After all, she did have a job to do, one that she'd been handling quite well until Cody marched through those big double doors.

She smiled and nodded at Andrea, sensing the return of her confidence. "All right, everybody," she said, her calm assurance belying the turmoil within. "Let's get back to work."

Cody was waiting in his office when Juliet looked for him at ten-fifteen.

"I'll leave the new pickup here. You can bring me back in the morning." He said it curtly; it was a mandate, as if she were his chauffeur rather than a friend who was giving him a ride in order that they might have time to talk. He stood up and began straightening a few papers on his desk, not even bothering to look up at her.

For a moment Juliet felt her shoulders slumping, as misery tried to creep up on her again. Cody had been her friend and champion for so long—and now he was treating her with such cold disregard. It hurt. Very much.

But then she realized that she honestly could think of nothing she'd done to make Cody behave this way. His nasty attitude had caught her off guard in the auditorium; she'd reacted to such hostility in her old way, going all numb and speechless. But she didn't have to keep acting like that. She *refused* to keep acting like that.

Juliet lifted her chin and said perkily, "Well, yes, Cody, I'd *love* to drive you into town tomorrow. It would be no problem for me at all. And, though you didn't bother to ask, we have just had an extremely successful audition, thank you. We have seven musical acts, two poets and every last part in each skit has been cast—not to mention Lalo Severin's performing poodle act and Raleigh McDuff's singing cat. Isn't that wonderful?"

Cody made a low growling sound in his throat, which Juliet decided to take as congratulations.

"Why, thank you. We are all extremely pleased. And everyone is especially thrilled that you will be taking part this year."

He did look up then, from under his brows. "Everyone's thrilled but you, right?"

He looked almost hurt. Lord, she had no idea of what to make of him lately. "Oh, Cody...."

He was insistent. "Right?"

She dropped the pretense of perkiness to answer frankly. "I had thought it would be better—it's true—if we weren't around each other so much. But that's not how it's turning out. So we'll just have to make the best of it, I suppose."

"Sure. We'll make the best of it." The words were heavy with sarcasm.

"Cody." She stared at him, bewildered, across the barrier of his desk. "What *is* the matter with you?"

"We'll talk about it," he said, coming around the desk toward her. "On the way home."

They went out to the old pickup that he'd lent her. She drove. They were barely out of McIntyre's parking lot, when all of a sudden he demanded, "Where did you get that dress?"

She glanced over at him. It was dark enough that she couldn't read anything in his face, but his tone had been nothing short of accusatory.

"At a department store, where else?" Her tone was bright, but with a slight brittle edge. She realized she was finally beginning to feel exasperated with him; it was a rare emotion for her, but one that was probably inevitable given the changes in her and the way he was acting. "Why? Is there something wrong with it?"

"It's red," he said, as if wearing red were some kind of capital offense.

She gave him another glance, wondering if perhaps there were something seriously wrong with him that was ruining his attitude and that he hadn't told her about yet—perhaps he had contracted a terminal disease, or had lost everything gambling in Tahoe and would soon be on the street. But, really, neither tragedy looked likely. He was the picture of health. And since she was his bookkeeper, she would probably already be aware of it if he had some sort of problem with gambling.

Maybe there *was* something wrong with the dress. She looked down at it briefly, but could see nothing that could cause him to scowl in such extreme disapproval. It had a scoop neck, no sleeves, a fitted drop waist and a full skirt. Perhaps it showed her figure more than the clothes she used to wear did, but it was hardly risqué.

"I like red," she said, quite reasonably.

"You never used to wear red," he grumbled. "Or high heels, either." He cast a disparaging frown at the floor-boards where her feet were.

That did it. They had just reached the two-lane highway that led to the ranch. Juliet spotted a place where the shoulder of the road looked wide enough and pulled off there.

"What the hell is this?" he demanded.

She ignored him until she'd safely parked the pickup beneath a big fir tree and turned off the engine and lights.

"Cody," she said then, letting her own hurt feelings show. "You are acting like someone I don't even know. I explained all about the changes I'm trying to make in my life. Why are you behaving as if I've done something *criminal?* I just don't understand it."

A logging truck rumbled by, close enough that its tail wind caused the pickup to rock just a little. "This is damn dangerous," Cody said.

"Then answer my question, and we'll leave."

"What question?"

"Why are you angry with me?"

"I'm not angry. Did I say I was angry?"

"No. You didn't have to. You haven't said a civil word to me since you came stomping into the auditorium and demanded that poor Archie withdraw from participation in the revue."

"*'Poor Archie,'*" he echoed, in a distinctly snarly tone. "There's nothing poor about Archie. I pay him union wages, and he makes damn good tips."

"I wasn't referring to the fatness of his wallet, Cody, and you know that, too. I mean poor as in pitiful. I felt sorry for him, the way you jumped on him."

"I didn't jump on him—exactly."

"You did so."

"And besides, he's not pitiful, believe me. All the women love him. Why do you think he wants to work days? Because he's always got a date at night, that's why."

"So what's wrong with that? Maybe he likes to have fun."

"Does he ever. Stay away from him."

"What?"

"He's not the guy for you. Don't get mixed up with him."

"But, Cody—"

"No buts. I'm dead serious."

"Cody—"

"He's all wrong for you."

Juliet squinted at Cody, across the darkness of the cab. "Well, I know that," she said.

He was quiet for a moment. Then he said "Uh...you do?"

She nodded, and then briskly explained, "What I'm after, in the long run, is a full life—one that includes meaningful work, good friends and good times. Eventually I plan to marry a nice man. Someone steady and true, with a good sense of humor and an ability to take life in stride. We'll have a family—two girls and a boy."

"You will?"

She nodded. Since Thursday, she'd been giving the matter some serious thought, especially at night, when she was trying not to think about Cody. "Archie—though I do like him a lot—isn't the man for me at all."

"He isn't?"

"No."

"Why not?"

"Well..."

"Because he's not steady and true?"

"Isn't he? I never thought about that."

"But you said the man in your life would have to be—"

"Steady and true. Yes I said that."

"So...?"

"So, I never got to the point of wondering that about Archie Kent."

"Why not?"

"Because it just...doesn't *happen* when I look at Archie."

"It?"

"Yes."

"What is *it?*"

What happens when I look at you, she thought, and blushed, then felt grateful for the darkness. She gestured rather awkwardly and hit her hand on the steering wheel. "Ouch," she said, instead of answering his question.

"Julie, you're making no sense at all," he said.

She held her bumped hand and observed, "Well, at least you're calling me Julie again."

He said nothing for a moment. And then he actually smiled. She saw the whiteness of his teeth in the dark. "Okay. I was a jerk."

"You were."

"I've made it a point all my life *not* to be a jerk."

"Up until recently, you've been a great success."

"I thought you were interested in Archie Kent. I was..."
He looked away, out the windshield, as if the fir tree were suddenly of great interest to him.

"You were what?" The question came out sounding frankly hopeful, which she hadn't intended at all.

He looked at her again, and then leaned toward her a little, so that his face came into sharper focus within the shadowed cab. She was imminently aware of him, of his big, lean body, so close. Of the warmth that emanated from him, and of the sudden, intense longing she had that he might lean closer still.

"Worried," he said, his voice paradoxically husky. "I was worried about you." His beautiful mouth formed the words.

"Worried. Why?" Her own voice sounded mildly dazed.

"I didn't want you to get hurt."

"Well, that's my problem, whether I get hurt."

"I know, but..." He didn't finish.

She didn't care that his voice trailed off into a sigh. She was busy remembering. . . .

Everything. About last Thursday night. As if it were happening right now, in fragments of glorious sensation....

The feel of his lips covering hers, the sweet fire that bloomed and rose as the kiss went on and on. The exquisite brush of his hand on her breast, and the way her nipple had pebbled up, becoming achingly sensitive, begging for more.

Now, just recalling it, she felt her nipples hardening again, though he wasn't even stroking them, though he wasn't touching her at all. She longed to lean forward, offer him her mouth and pray that he would take it.

But she didn't. She reminded herself that, in spite of the way *it* happened whenever Cody McIntyre looked her way lately, he was no more the man for her than Archie Kent was. With a hunk like Cody, *it* wouldn't last forever. She'd lose him eventually to some more desirable woman. And she'd end up with a broken heart.

No, she knew she would be better off to wait for the right man. Someone less beautiful than Cody, someone less *everything* than Cody. But someone she could count on. She would seek a balance—steady and true, first and foremost. And with at least a smidgen of *it* to make life worthwhile.

The thought made her suddenly sad. To end up settling for a smidgen, when with Cody she could probably experience a hugeness, an immensity of *it*....

Cody murmured her name then, softly. And she realized she'd leaned toward him as he was leaning toward her. A wonderful, voluptuous feeling came over her—a melting sort of feeling. How delicious it would be to just dissolve right into Cody's arms.

But that would only be asking for trouble. She caught herself, with a little shudder, and withdrew to a safer distance against the door.

A funny expression crossed his face, one that almost looked like regret or hurt—that she'd backed away? But then she told herself it was just wishful thinking. She couldn't see very well in the darkness anyway.

They were both quiet for a moment. Another big truck went by, rocking the cab.

She remembered what they'd been talking about before *it* intervened. "Well, if you think Archie's wrong for me, that's okay. I think so, too. And so does Archie, more than likely. There's really nothing between us."

He gave a low laugh. "Okay. I'm convinced."

"So can he be in the revue?"

"Why not?"

"Great. Now take back the mean remarks you made about my dress, and we can go home."

"I don't know," he replied, and she was glad for the humor in his tone. "That dress is...downright red. And what would your mother say if she saw you in it?"

Juliet thought of her mother; it helped to settle her down a little, soothed her dangerous desire to keep on flirting when what she should be doing was starting the engine and getting them home—to their separate houses.

She admitted, "My mother brought me up to be reserved and old-fashioned, it's true. But lately she's changed...."

Since he'd met her mother more than once over the years, Cody made a small disbelieving sound, though he didn't actually comment. They looked at each other for a moment, and the subject of Juliet's mother became the last thing on either of their minds.

Finally Cody said in a hesitant voice that touched and vibrated something in Juliet's heart, "Julie... I haven't liked this. The way you've been keeping away from me. I thought..."

"Yes?" There it was, that high, hopeful note again, in her own voice.

"I thought, when you shocked the hell out of us all and got up in front of the association last week, that it was kind of sad. The way we've known each other all our lives, the way we call each other friends, live a few hundred yards apart—and yet we don't *really* know each other."

Juliet considered that. "Yes. I see what you mean. I've always been so shy. And you looked out for me, took care of me, more than anything else."

"Yeah, I guess," he said, and then struggled for a moment to arrange his thoughts. "But, at least in the past you never actually *avoided* me. Hell, what I'm trying to say is, even if we never were real close, I did consider us friends, longtime friends. And since Thursday, I feel like—" he dragged in a breath "—I feel like I've lost a friend."

"Oh, Cody. I'm sorry."

"Look," he went on, "if you don't think I'm the right kind of guy for you, that's okay. I can deal with that. But, damn it, Julie. I *miss* you. Can't you be my friend again?"

"Oh, Cody...." She didn't know what to say. There was a lump in her throat that she had to swallow before she could even begin to explain. "I just thought it would be better, for a while," she managed to say at last, "to stay away from each other."

He said nothing for a moment, then looked out his side window. "Right. I figured that."

And she knew she could no longer continue to reject such a friend as he was. As he'd always been. Eventually, she was sure, this new and frightening attraction she felt for him would pass. And then it would be a pure pleasure to be friends again.

But for the sake of the hundred and one ways he'd always been there for her over the years, she wasn't going to deny their friendship now.

"All right." She smiled. "Avoiding you doesn't seem to have done much good anyway. I'm through with that. As of now."

He looked at her then. "Thanks, Julie," he said. Her silly heart seemed to turn over in response to the flash of his teeth in the darkness.

She drew a deep breath and ordered her heart to stop racing like that. It would all work out fine, she told herself. This crazy attraction was just a passing thing. Not surprising at all, when she considered all the changes she'd been going through of late. She'd set a goal of becoming more assertive, and going after her goal had set in motion some other changes. She was...awakening as a woman. And Cody had helped her along in that awakening—with those incredible kisses the other night.

But this was real life, not *Sleeping Beauty*. Cody might look like a handsome prince, but that was as far as the fairy tale went in this case. A kiss, these days, rarely signified the start of a lifetime's commitment. And just because what they'd done had thrilled her to her toes didn't mean she was in love with him or anything.

No, it had been a...physical reaction, that was all. And she would always be grateful to Cody for doing such a marvelous job of showing her what all the hoopla was about when it came to this mysterious and remarkable thing that went on between men and women.

Cody reached across the cab to briefly squeeze her hand. "I'm glad we talked," he said.

"Me, too." Her voice cracked a little, because his touch, quick and light as it was, created a chain reaction. From the point of contact, an electrical jolt shot right down into the center of her, where it struck a spark that heated everything up and began a minor internal meltdown.

Juliet started the pickup and concentrated on getting back out on the road and home to the ranch.

Soon enough, she told herself soothingly, as she waited for the meltdown to pass and her body to settle down, this won't happen every time he comes near me. Soon enough, everything will be like it was before.

She had no idea that Cody, smiling contentedly on his side of the cab, saw things in a slightly different light. He really was grateful that they were no longer going to be staying out of each other's way. And it *had* been bothering him that they'd been friends for so long and yet always maintained a certain distance with each other.

To Cody, right now seemed the perfect time for them to become much better friends than they had ever been before.

Five

Juliet had just rolled over and banged on her alarm to make it be quiet, when the knock came at the kitchen door.

"Uugh," she muttered, and tried to make the world go away by covering her head with her pillow. But the knock came again.

She sat up. "All right! Just a minute."

She was just belting her light robe over her sleep-wrinkled pajamas when she threw back the door.

"Morning." Cody grinned at her. He wore old jeans and a plaid shirt and his most ancient pair of rawhide boots. To Juliet, he looked even better than he had the night before when he'd burst through the double doors of the auditorium and demanded that Archie Kent back out of the revue. Yes, she thought sleepily, covering a yawn with the back of her hand. It really was true. He kept getting better looking every time she saw him.

She peered at him, still half asleep, wondering vaguely if she looked as rumpled and groggy as she felt, telling herself it shouldn't bother her if she did.

She heard panting and a thumping sound and managed to stop staring at Cody's incredible face long enough to glance down at his dog. Kemo sat beside Cody, looking up at her, his mouth open and his tongue lolling cheerfully to one side.

Cody gestured vaguely at the barn and stables beyond the fence. "I was just doing the morning chores."

Juliet nodded. "Oh. Right. The chores."

"Yeah. And I thought—"

"Hmm?"

"Well, I thought I'd just drop by and invite you over to the house for breakfast."

"Breakfast."

"Yeah. You know. Eggs. Bacon. Toast. Coffee."

"You want me to come over for breakfast."

He started combing his hair with his fingers. "Well, yeah." He looked down at his dog, who made a little whine that actually sounded like encouragement, and then he looked back at her. "How about it?"

She didn't answer for a moment. She was thinking that not avoiding him was one thing, having breakfast with him another. "Well, Cody..." she began, wondering how to tell him no without hurting him.

His face fell. "No?" he asked flatly. "You won't come?"

"Cody, I—"

He put up a hand. "Never mind. It was only a thought." He turned away, and she felt totally heartless, in spite of the emotional danger he represented, to reject him this way.

"Wait."

He turned back. "Yeah?"

"Give me twenty minutes to get myself together."

His face lit up. "Great." He slapped his thigh in a signal to the dog, and left without another word.

Juliet stared after him for a moment, slightly stupefied that he had asked her over for breakfast—and that she had accepted. Then it came to her that in twenty minutes she had to be showered, dressed and ready to eat. So she closed the door and flew toward the bathroom, shedding her robe and pajamas as she went.

Cody, who had changed into a newer pair of jeans and a fresh shirt, had the food almost ready when Juliet knocked on the door. He led her to the kitchen and gestured toward a chair in the breakfast nook, which looked out on the open field where two of his horses were grazing. He poured her coffee and asked how she liked her eggs, and then he fried them and set the meal before her, slipping into a chair across from her after that.

Juliet drank some coffee, picked up her fork, ate half an egg and then asked the question she'd been pondering all the time she showered and dressed. "Cody, what is this all about?"

He stopped in the middle of munching a slice of bacon. "What?" He looked extremely innocent.

"This. You having me over for breakfast all of a sudden."

He shrugged. "I don't know. It seemed like a nice idea. So I invited you."

"But we never do things like this together."

"Like what?" he challenged, then went on without waiting for her answer. "We have lunch together now and then."

"Business lunches."

"Food's food," he said.

"Wrong." She munched a little bacon herself and then she accused, "And you know it, too. A business lunch is a far cry from cooking for someone in your own kitchen."

"You mean you appreciate my efforts?" he asked, missing the point entirely.

"Well, of course I do—"

She didn't get to qualify her statement by explaining that perhaps sharing breakfast was a little more than what they should be doing together right now, because he grinned widely—presumably in appreciation of *her* appreciation—and her heart distracted her, going all rambunctious for a moment. He looked her over, and beneath her conservative suit, her whole body tingled.

"Hey," he said. "I like that suit."

Juliet, who still hadn't explained that they couldn't be spending *too* much time together, after all, glanced down at the outfit in question and wondered what he saw to like about it. She'd bought it several months ago, before she'd made her birthday vow. The cut was undistinguished, and the color was called "wheat." "Wheat" sounded nice when the clerk at the department store described it. "Just your color, my dear. A lovely, subtle wheat...." But when Juliet got the suit home, she realized the truth; "wheat" was just another name for brown—a sort of watered-down brown, actually.

Juliet finished contemplating the bland suit and looked up at Cody once more. "I hate this suit," she said, with perhaps more malice than was called for. "But I'm still practical enough that I'm not willing to get rid of it. I don't know what you can possibly see in it."

He pondered for a moment, then said thoughtfully, "I don't know. Maybe it kind of...reassures me that you're still a little bit the Julie I used to know."

He reached across then, so swiftly that she had no opportunity to move back, and snared her hand where it lay on the edge of the table. His touch was warm and enveloping. All coherent thought fled her mind. Slowly he pulled her nearer, across the barrier of the table between them.

"*Are* you still the same Julie?" he asked, in a hushed, breath-held kind of tone.

"I...um, certainly, to a certain extent, yes...."

He smiled, then, because her voice itself had proved she told the truth. It had broken on a gasp between the *y* and *e* of *yes,* just the way it used to before.

"Good," he said, and released her.

Her hand felt hot. Her wrist, where he'd held it, tingled deliciously. She stared at him, unable to utter a word.

He lifted his coffee cup and gestured with it. "Eat your food before it gets cold." He returned to his own meal with gusto.

Juliet continued to stare at him a bit longer, waiting for the tingling that had spread from her hand to her whole body to subside. At last, when she felt she was more or less back to normal again, she realized she was starved and eagerly dug back into the meal.

She looked up just as she was polishing off her second piece of toast to find him watching her. She cast about for a way to explain how things like this breakfast shouldn't happen again for a while.

But before she found the words, he wiped his mouth with his napkin and asked, "So tell me about your mother."

Her mouth was open—she'd been just about to speak. She closed it and gave him a baffled frown. "My mother?"

"Last night," he elaborated, "you said she's changed."

Juliet raised her cup to her lips and realized there was nothing in there. So she stood up, went to the coffeepot, and returned to fill their cups. Unfortunately, she hadn't thought about how close she'd have to stand to him to give him more coffee until she was already at his side. She poured, poignantly aware of the solid warmth of him, the silky rust-colored hairs on the back of his hands and the gleam in his eyes.

"Julie?" He was grinning up at her.

"Um, yes?" She realized his cup was full and brought the pot upright just in time.

"I asked you about your mother."

"My mother."

"If she'd changed."

Juliet cleared her throat. "Right. My mother. She has. Changed."

He looked doubtful. "Since when?"

She ordered her legs to carry her away from him, back to the counter to return the pot to the warming plate. As soon as she gained a little distance from him, she found it was easier to think about the question he'd just asked. "She's changed since she and Dad sold the antique store."

"Changed how?"

Juliet stayed there at the counter for a moment, leaning back against it. Putting aside the nagging voice of her wiser self that urged she tell Cody she wouldn't be having break-fast with him again soon, she considered his question. "My mother's ... relaxed her standards a little, I'd say. She isn't as prudish and proper as she used to be. Until they sold the store, it kind of defined them. They'd owned it for so long, since way before I was born...."

Thinking of the antique store, Juliet found herself caught up in memories of it. As a child, she'd spent long hours in the musty old brick building that had been an assay office during the gold rush. Her memories of those years seemed mostly to consist of her parents urging her to "hush"—and to be careful of this or that priceless heirloom. Her parents had been older, in their early forties when she was born. They were a quiet, retiring pair, set in their ways.

She went on, musingly, "Yes, they defined themselves by that store. And then, when they finally sold it, they began to look at the world in a different way."

"What way?"

"I don't know, more open-mindedly, I suppose...." Juliet stared out the window beyond the table, but she wasn't really seeing the big, wide field. She was seeing herself as a solitary little girl, an only child who quivered at the prospect of trying to make a friend, whose aging parents had interests way beyond her childish comprehension.

"Julie? You all right?" Cody's voice was edged with concern.

"Yes, yes. Just thinking."

"About what?"

She shifted her glance from the open field to Cody's face. "My father used to call me 'Little Mouse.' Did you know that?" Cody shook his head. She went on, "He meant it affectionately, but eventually I kind of began to feel like one. Like a little mouse hiding in the dusty junk left over from other people's lives...." Totally without her permission, a single tear trickled down her cheek. Juliet's voice faded off.

"Julie...." His tone was soft.

She swiped the tear away. "Don't worry. Just indulging in a little self-pity. But I'm through now." Her voice became brisk as she continued, "I think the difference in my mother is partly due to Hawaii." After they sold the antique store, her parents had bought a condominium on the island of Maui and they'd retired there.

"I guess," he conceded wryly, "that Hawaii might have a certain effect, even on your mother."

"You never did like my mother," she remarked a little sourly, coming back to the table and reclaiming her chair.

"No," he contended. "*She* never did like *me*."

"That's not true." Juliet regretted how unconvincing she sounded.

"Oh, isn't it? Then what about that time I brought you home after Billy Butley tore your dress and pushed you into Nugget Creek? She immediately assumed I was the one who did it."

"I straightened her out."

"Not until after she told me never to come near you again."

"She took that back."

"Only because she couldn't do otherwise."

"Oh, Cody. She could just never understand why someone like you would look out for a mouse like me. She was suspicious."

"Of what?"

"Well, that you were...up to no good."

"How?"

Juliet felt her face coloring and hesitated before answering.

Cody figured it out for himself before she spoke. He choked on his coffee as awareness dawned. "She thought I was out to *seduce* you?"

Juliet nodded. "It's silly, I know." She hastened to add, "But she doesn't feel that way anymore."

He gave her a disbelieving frown. "You're just saying that."

"No. On my honor, it's true. After all, there were all those years where you dated so...widely. And people do talk, after all. When she found out you had so many girl-friends, she decided there wasn't much likelihood you'd be needing to take advantage of *me*. And now, since Hawaii, well, she and my dad both have loosened up a lot. As a matter of fact," Juliet went on as proof positive of the change in her mother, "when she called last week, she mentioned that she's bought a bikini."

"Emma Huddleston. In a bikini?" Cody sounded frankly incredulous.

"People *can* change."

Cody said gruffly, "Tell me something I don't already know."

He was looking at her in a very focused, intense way. Outside, she heard the roar of a lawn mower starting up. The loud sound made her jump, as she thought of what he'd done a few minutes before, taking her hand, pulling her closer, making her long to get closer still.

This was all playing with fire, and she knew it. It had not been wise to come into his house and share breakfast with him. Certainly, they'd been friends forever and a day—but distant friends, with strictly proscribed limits on their relationship. It made no sense at all to go expanding the boundaries of their friendship right now, when she quivered clear down to her toes every time he so much as smiled at her. But somehow, every time she tried to tell him how she felt about all this, he either melted her with a look, or changed the subject before she even had a chance to begin.

She decided grimly that talking to him about this wasn't going to work. It was action that was called for. Breakfast was over, and she would see that a situation like this didn't arise again until this...*crush* she had on Cody was no more than a sweet, distant memory.

She stood up. "You know, it's probably time we got going. I should be over at McMulch's Lumberyard by nine." She added, unnecessarily, "I'm doing a unit cost analysis for them."

"Oh, yeah. Sure." He stood up, too, and started carrying things to the sink. She helped him.

All was in order in no time. They went out together, got in the old pickup that she'd parked in the front drive and started for town, waving at the old caretaker, Bud Southey, who was out on the riding mower cutting the six acres of grass when they left.

Juliet was careful to keep the talk away from anything personal as they drove. They agreed she could just leave the old pickup in the lot behind McIntyre's if her car was through at the shop. She told him that since he wasn't in any of the skits, he probably wouldn't be called on to rehearse for the revue until the last few days before opening, when they put the whole thing together.

When she left him at Emerald Gap Hardware, she thanked him for the breakfast.

"My pleasure," he said. "Anytime."

She smiled and nodded and tried not to pay any heed to the way her heart fluttered inside her chest, and her skin got too warm and her breath hitched and caught.

He left, turning once to wave before going in the hardware store's back door, and when he was gone she grimly muttered, "'Anytime,' hah. Not anytime soon...."

Cody, though, had meant exactly what he had said. Breakfast with Julie *had* been a pure pleasure. And he intended to make sure the pleasure was repeated soon.

Whistling, he entered the narrow, cramped storeroom behind the hardware store that his father had built. There was nobody there yet. The store didn't open until ten.

He busied himself making the coffee that he provided for his employees, and when it was through dripping, he poured himself a cup. Then he went out to the floor safe beneath the register in the store itself, and took the money and receipts to the back again to tally up. The take, he discovered, hadn't been bad for a Monday.

He felt pleased, much more than the few extra bucks he was looking at warranted.

Still whistling, he put the money in a leather bag and waited for Elma Lou Bealer, who would open up. When she arrived, he exchanged a few pleasantries, unlocked the register and took the leather bag the half block to the back entrance of McIntyre's.

Inside the restaurant, which was also deserted, since it didn't open until eleven, he repeated the process of counting the money earned the day before.

He had to count twice, because Julie's image kept superimposing itself over the faces of Washington, Lincoln and Jackson. When he was done, he put the restaurant's money into the leather bag with the cash from the store and glanced up at the big clock on the office wall; it was nearly ten.

He went out to his truck and drove to the bank, where he didn't even have to wait in line for the merchant's window. By ten-fifteen, the money was safely deposited. He went back to the restaurant to go over the meat order with the head chef.

From noon to a little before two, he stayed at the restaurant, playing host, overseeing things. After that, he stopped in at the hardware store to discuss housewares and garden stock with a local salesman.

Before he knew it, it was dinnertime. He wondered if Julie had eaten yet. She probably would be working tonight on the festival, either at the auditorium or down at the town hall. It was very important that she take time to eat.

He went back to the restaurant and ordered two meals of halibut steak with new potatoes and string beans and carrots almondine. Lots of protein and fresh vegetables. Very important for a woman working overtime. When the prep man packed it up for him, he had him add a nice bottle of wine.

Just before six, he parked his pickup in front of the refurbished Victorian building where Julie rented office space. Then he carried the big basket of food inside.

He was in luck. She was there, her office door open. He could hear the printer of her computer, making quick, low hissing sounds as it printed something. She was sitting at her desk.

He set the basket down and knocked on the door frame. "Julie?"

She looked up from the spread sheets she was studying. He had the feeling that he kept having lately whenever he looked into her eyes—like the floor had dropped out from under him for a moment. She blinked. "Cody?"

He said, "Julie," and then stood there for a few minutes grinning like an idiot. Then he remembered the basket. He bent, hoisted it and held it out, offering it proudly. "I thought you might be hungry, so I had Roger grill us a couple of halibut steaks."

She stared for a moment. Then she said, "Oh, Cody," as if he'd done something he shouldn't have.

"What?" He felt like a fool all of a sudden, standing there with a big picnic basket, when a minute before it had seemed like a completely logical thing to do—to bring dinner for her.

Her printer finished printing. The graceful old building seemed very quiet.

"Come in," she said. "Close the door."

He brought the basket beyond the threshold and turned to shut out the hallway. Then he sat in one of the two wing chairs across from her desk and looked down at the gray slacks that he'd changed in to in his office before coming over here.

"Cody, I can't handle this," she said. Her soft voice broke once, in the middle of *can't,* the way it used to do all the time, before she started becoming someone he couldn't stop thinking about.

He decided to try to lighten the mood. "Can't handle what? You hate halibut?"

She didn't even crack a smile. "I agreed to stop avoiding you, not to spend every spare moment with you."

That hurt. "You don't like to spend time with me?"

"I do like it, Cody. I like it too much."

"So what's wrong with that?"

"A lot."

"Why?"

"Oh, Cody...."

"*Oh, Cody,* tells me nothing."

"Oh, Cody...."

He waited.

Finally she managed, "I explained it, last Thursday night. Eventually, I'd be the one to get hurt, if you and I...got involved."

"Who says we're getting involved?" She chose not even to answer that and just gave him a frustrated frown. So he went on. "And, if we did, who says you'd get hurt? Maybe *I'd* get hurt. Hell, maybe *neither* of us would get hurt. Did you ever think of that?"

"Oh, Cody. Be realistic. Look at you. Look at me. It's obvious who'd end up with the broken heart when it was over."

Something inside him snapped then. He stood up in a quick, angry motion. She shrank back in her swivel chair. "That's the dumbest damn notion I've ever heard," he growled. "I *have* looked at you, and you look just fine."

And she did, too, with her fair hair around her shoulders, and her hazel eyes wide. There were two warm spots of color high on her cheeks. And she'd taken off the jacket of that nice suit she said she hated and gone and unbuttoned the top buttons of her blouse again.

She looked...like a woman who ought to be kissed. And Cody was damn willing to take on the job. He came around the desk. She watched him come, her eyes widening even more. When the desk no longer separated them, he stood looking down at her.

"Cody...."

He decided not to say a damn thing. She'd only start arguing with him again, and she talked too much anyway, lately. He bent down to her, putting his arms on her chair arms, bringing his face level with hers.

Her wide eyes relaxed a little, then, as she lowered her eyelids to look at his mouth. "Cody...."

Since she seemed so interested in his mouth, he moved it a little closer, so that he could feel her warm, sweet breath as it sighed in and out.

"Oh, Cody...."

He wrapped his hands around her arms and straightened up very slowly, pulling her with him. Then he gathered her close and took her mouth with his own.

Six

For Juliet, the meltdown began.

Cody's lips played over hers and his arms held her tight and all she could think of was that she hoped he would never stop. He nudged her lips apart with gentle urgings, and his tongue darted in and...oh, down in her abdomen, there was a slow-spreading heat that made her feel all liquid and yearning for more.

His hands strayed up and down, touching and stroking the entire of her back from the gentle flare of her hips, up over the curve of her waist, and out to her shoulders. Pulling her nearer, he caressed her neck and then held her head still, one firm hand along each cheek, so his mouth could torment her even more thoroughly than it had done up till now.

She groaned, an utterly abandoned sound, and her head fell back. He cradled her head then, with one hand, while he combed her hair in long, sweet strokes with the fingers of the other hand, lifting his mouth from hers enough to whisper low, seductive things that made her blush at the same time as she longed to hear more.

And then, once again, he was kissing her, slanting his lips one way and then the other, trailing little love bites down her neck, and then kissing her collarbone, which tingled deliciously at such sensuous attention.

His hand slid up and under the silk of her white blouse, pushing it aside as he touched her bare skin. The tiny white buttons of the blouse, moored loosely, slipped free of their holes and the blouse gaped a little, exposing her plain white slip.

"Oh my goodness," she murmured, just as she had last Thursday night. And she felt the blouse glide down over one shoulder.

Cody's warm, big hand slid beneath the strap of her plain slip, guiding it gently over the swell of her shoulder, until it fell down her arm, pulling one side of the slip with it, and exposing one cup of the lacy push-up bra she'd bought on a shopping spree in Sacramento a few weeks before.

He pulled away a little, and looked down at the soft swell of her breast nestled in the lace of the new bra. "Pretty." He sighed, and his hand drifted lower, until he cupped the small mound.

Juliet looked down, too, experiencing a most wondrous, languorous feeling. She watched as his thumb teased her nipple through the lace and felt the nipple grow hard and protruding. Then he slipped his thumb under the lace, and he guided the lace beneath the swell of her breast, so the nipple was revealed.

"Oh, Cody...." She moaned aloud, and her head dropped back. He caught her on his free arm.

Then he lowered his mouth and kissed her exposed breast, first with little brushing, breathy kisses. Then, his lips finding the hard nipple, he licked it and blew on it and at last took it inside his mouth.

Oh, it felt lovely when he kissed her that way. Juliet's senses whirled madly as he suckled on her breast. Nothing half so wonderful had ever happened to her in her entire thirty years. And when he pushed down the slip on the other side, and got the bra out of the way there, too, she thought perhaps she had tumbled out of the real world into some alternate universe—a realm of the senses, where pleasure thrilled and consumed and nothing mattered but the delicious torment of Cody's lips on her burning skin.

And then, out in the hall, she heard the rumble of the janitor's cleaning cart. And she realized where she was.

"Oh, my Lord...." she murmured.

Cody must have sensed the sudden unwelcome tension in her body, because he stopped doing those incredible things to her bare breasts and lifted his head enough that their eyes could meet. His gaze was hot, heavy-lidded with desire.

He said, very low, "You want me to stop?"

For a brief eternity, she had no words to answer him. Since the moment he pulled her slowly from her swivel chair, it hadn't occurred to her that there was any possibility of stopping this marvelous, frightening thing that was happening between them. It all seemed ... inevitable. Like the sun setting at night, only to rise again with the dawn.

While she dazedly contemplated his question, he made the decision for her.

"This isn't the place," he muttered. And began putting her clothing to rights, the gentleness of his hands belying the grim set of his jaw.

After staring at him dumbly for a few seconds more, she bestirred herself and helped him. It took no time at all, and her breasts were once again properly covered with bra, slip and blouse.

But Juliet herself felt completely naked. As the seconds passed, she found it more and more difficult to look at Cody, who now seemed a silent and forbidding presence— first right in front of her, and then, as he quietly moved away, on the other side of her desk.

When she made herself sit down and forced herself to look at him, she realized he was unpacking the basket of food he had brought.

He caught her eye, and she thought she detected a spark of anger in his look. If there was, she couldn't really blame him, as there were so many inconsistencies in her behavior lately. She kept saying things like they couldn't spend so much time together—and then melting in his arms the moment he touched her.

"It's getting cold," he said of the food. "No sense wasting it."

She didn't know what to do right then, so she let him feed her for the second time that day, watching numbly as he cleared the papers off of her desk, laid place mats and set out the covered plates. He even poured wine.

She ate without really tasting, though she was obscurely aware that the food was excellent. She hadn't much appetite after what had just happened, but she knew her body needed fuel to get through the evening meeting with her committee chairpeople that lay ahead.

Once, in the course of the silent meal, the janitor rapped on the door. Juliet called to him that they would be finished soon, and he moved on down the hall.

When they were both done and Cody was repacking the basket, Juliet thanked him for the dinner. The words sounded awkward and falsely social, dropping from her lips into the cavernous silence that now yawned between them. The intimacy of his touch had been too shattering this time. It had made even the stunningly erotic kiss of last Thursday seem like child's play by comparison. Now, thanking him for the dinner was little more than meaningless noise-making—a polite sound to cover the demolished state of her nerves.

"You're welcome." He gave the empty pleasantry right back as he lifted the basket and strode to the door.

Just before he pulled the door open, she found some small reserve of courage that she'd feared had deserted her. "Cody."

He stopped without turning. "Yeah."

"In spite of the way I acted when you kissed me, I meant what I said. I don't want to get involved with you in a...romantic way."

"Why did I know you would say that?" He spoke with resigned irony.

"Do I have to start avoiding you again?"

He didn't answer for a moment. Then his sculpted shoulders lifted in an eloquent shrug. "Hell, no." He turned to face her. "Don't worry. I'm no genius, but I think I got your message this time. If you're still willing to tell me no after what happened a little while ago, then I'm willing to believe you really mean it. Don't bother to avoid me, Julie. Because I'll be avoiding you." He turned away again and pulled open the door. The janitor was once more approaching in the hall. "Come on in," Cody said, stepping beyond the threshold. "We're finished in here."

Cody was a man who meant what he said. For over a week Juliet caught no more than passing glimpses of him—on the street, or early in the morning, when he went out to feed the animals. Twice, late at night, when the demons of forbidden desire were at their most devilish, he gifted her with impromptu concerts from the porch of the main house.

No one would ever know how difficult it was for her to stay in her bed at those times. She, who'd always been too timid to even dislike anyone, almost hated Cody McIntyre when he played those beautiful songs on the harmonica, and she pictured his mouth making the music happen, and remembered what his mouth had done to her.

She tossed and turned. But somehow, by grimly reminding herself that she wanted more from the first man she made love with than unparalleled ecstasy and an eventual broken heart, she managed to stay where she was.

Her car—which the man at the garage had sworn, with a bit of a smirk, was as good as new—offered some solace. She found great comfort in putting on something red and driving the mountain roads a little faster than she should have, feeling the powerful engine purring at her command. She'd roll all the windows down and open the sunroof when she drove like that, letting the wind play with her hair. And she'd only slow down when it became impossible not to imagine Cody's hands, playing with her hair—and every other part of her, for that matter.

And, thank heaven, there was the festival to take up so much of her spare time that there weren't many opportunities for dreaming about a man she couldn't have anyway.

Midsummer Madness was shaping up marvelously. For the revue, the little play about Maria Elena, starring Yolanda and Archie, was nothing short of grand melodrama, and even the poodle act looked like fun. Reva Reid, chairperson of the Opening Day Parade committee, had signed up a record of thirty-five different floats. And Burt Pandley had already filled the town hall with more crafts and industry booths than they'd had any previous year.

Flat-nosed Jake, who was always full of surprises, had a friend on the staff of the *Sacramento Bee*. The friend had come to visit, and it looked as if there was going to be a cover story about the festival in the *Bee*'s Sunday supplement on the twenty-first, the Sunday before the festival began. Everyone was thrilled. Even Babe Allen, who'd groused about having to pay a director's fee when Juliet wasn't a true professional, had changed her tune; twice she'd mentioned ways they could expand further on a good thing *next* year—when, of course, Juliet would be handling things once more, wouldn't she?

If it weren't for this craving for Cody that wouldn't go away, Juliet's life would have been just about as perfect as she ever might have imagined in her wildest fantasies of prospective assertiveness. But the craving to have Cody's arms around her was always there, underlying everything, even her triumph as festival director.

Sometimes, she'd try to think of her burning desire as a good thing, a sort of learning experience of the senses. She'd tell herself that what she was going through was a long-overdue sensual awakening—and then she'd want to scream because the man she longed for to help her wake up all the way would only cause her heartache in the end.

Sunday, the twenty-first, arrived. And with it came the front-page article about the festival in the Encore section of the *Sacramento Bee*. The cover of the supplement featured a full-page color photograph of the brick-fronted Gap Auditorium, hung from end-to-end with a huge banner announcing Midsummer Madness. The Victorian gaslights on the sidewalk, hinting nostalgically of another era, framed the shot.

Juliet, who got up at five and stationed herself outside the supermarket to wait for the papers to be delivered, bought ten copies.

In the article, Juliet was mentioned four times—and quoted twice. The writer described her as "this year's festival director, a local bookkeeper with a calm, no-nonsense air and a knack for getting the job done." Juliet was so thrilled that she clipped a copy of the article and sent it to her parents on Maui. Her mother called to congratulate her a few days later, saying that she and Juliet's father were impressed and excited with their daughter's success.

"Oh, Juliet, I knew it," her mother said just before she hung up. "I knew that you were changing, getting outside yourself, making the most of your life. And I'm so terribly grateful. The truth is that your father and I were rather... preoccupied parents, not to mention somewhat stuffy and judgmental—no, no, don't be sweet and say it's not true. We'd gotten in a rut as a childless couple, and we never really adapted to the changes that happened when you came along. We...kept you down, in a way. Wanted you quiet and untroublesome, above everything else. You gave us exactly what we asked for—a shy mouse.... Remember, that's what your father used to call you?"

"Yes," Juliet said softly. "I remember."

"But lately I've noticed several signs that you're becoming more outgoing. And when we received this clipping, well, I knew for sure that I'd been right. I think it's perfectly splendid of you. I truly do."

Juliet, feeling extremely emotional, managed to murmur a thank-you.

"Don't thank me. Thank yourself. You've done it all, I know."

They talked for a few minutes more, her mother enthusing about the breathtaking beauty of Maui and the spectacular black-sand beaches she and Juliet's father had visited on the big island recently.

At last Emma said, "And now I must go. Your father's waiting for me—our morning swim, you know."

Juliet pictured her seventy-two-year-old mother in her new bikini, and smiled as she said goodbye.

She sat for a while in bed after she hung up the phone, basking in her mother's approving words. She *had* come a long way since the day she'd turned thirty, and she resolved to keep in mind, whenever the vagaries of life got her down, all the strides she'd made.

Her resolve was tested that very evening, at the first of two dress rehearsals before the opening of the Midsummer Madness Revue, which was slated to kick off the festivities that Friday night.

Because everyone in the revue was working on a volunteer basis, Juliet had kept the time each act had to rehearse at a minimum by never scheduling a complete run-through until the last two rehearsals before opening night. This was time-saving overall, but made for a pair of grueling evenings when it finally came down to the wire. Not only did the set changes and act shifts have to be added in, but the lights and sound had to be used in sequence for the first time, too.

By two hours into the Wednesday night run-through— and less than halfway through the first act—tempers were generally on simmer up to boil. One of Lalo Severin's poodles had chased Raleigh McDuff's singing cat around the stage, finally treeing it on the act curtain. The cat then had to be coaxed down with a can of sardines, and the poodle was taken to where Andrea Oakleaf could administer first aid to the several long scratches on its nose. Yolanda Hughes, who had begun to show signs of artistic temperament, was in a rage over her costume, which she claimed bound her about the bust. Archie Kent was late. And two of the four Barbershop Boys had sore throats.

Juliet was beginning to feel the tension herself, trying to direct Yolanda through her death scene, while the bit players who were supposed to be the crazed members of a

bloodthirsty mob kept wandering offstage and returning
with cans of soda pop or boxes of cheese crackers.

"*Adiós, amigos.... Adiós amigas,*" Yolanda gallantly
intoned—and then started fiddling with the front of her
dress, muttering invectives against its faulty design.

Somehow, Yolanda stopped fidgeting long enough to be
effectively hung. But then the doleful music, meant to sig-
nify the passing of a blameless soul, did not come on. And
the single spot which was supposed to narrow down onto her
slowly swinging figure, somehow ended up on Bobby
Dumphy, down left, drinking a cola and munching a candy
bar.

Juliet felt so discouraged, she wanted to cry.

"Could I make a suggestion?" The voice came, rich and
low, into her ear.

Cody. Juliet stiffened. She'd seen him come in and sit in
the back to wait for his turn to perform. But then she'd
firmly blocked him from her mind.

She turned her head. Even in the dim light that bled from
the misplaced spotlight on stage, he looked wonderful.

"What?" she asked flatly.

"Hey, Juliet, what now?" someone demanded from up
on the stage; the mob was becoming restless.

"Help Yolanda down, bring up the lights and everybody
take five," Juliet instructed.

The lights came on, greeted by a halfhearted cheer from
the disbanding mob. Archie, who'd finally arrived, helped
the hangman to lower the swinging Yolanda.

Juliet shifted in her seat to face the object of her strictly
forbidden fantasies. "What's your suggestion?"

He answered with calm assurance. "Send everybody
home but the technical people. Then run it through—twice,
if possible—with just the lights and sound and set changes.
Have a few volunteers stick around to stand in the right

places for light changes. Then, tomorrow, when you've got the technical side down pat, you can add the performers, and it should go reasonably well.''

Juliet considered his suggestion—and had to admit it made better sense than trying to do everything at once. The performers, at least, already had a good idea of where they were supposed to be and how to get there. If she could just bring the lights and sound up to par, they might be all right.

''Good idea,'' she said after a moment. ''Thanks.''

''No problem,'' he said, and then went back up the aisle without another word. Juliet stared after him for a moment, thinking that even now, when she'd told him to stay away from her, he still came to her aid when she needed help. She knew sadness and longing then, which she couldn't afford to examine. So she forced herself to face front again, before he disappeared through the double doors.

''All right, everyone!'' she announced. ''If I could have your attention for a moment. . . .''

Cody's plan worked well, all things considered. The lights and sound ran like clockwork the next night, and the performers did much better at holding up their end. The poodle once more growled at the singing cat, and Yolanda, who'd altered her costume herself, still was not pleased. But Archie Kent was on time, and all four Barbershop Boys were ready to sing ''Sweet Adeline'' in harmony.

Cody, who treated Juliet with distant politeness, sang a rollicking tune about a cowboy and a splay-shanked mule in the first act. His other number, in the second act, was a new one, a ballad. Juliet was called backstage just as it started it, so she didn't hear the song itself. But he was playing the final chords on his twelve-string when she returned. After the last note faded, there was silence, and then even Bobby Dumphy stopped eating long enough to applaud.

That final rehearsal ended near 1:00 a.m., but everyone left in high spirits. The revue wasn't perfect by a long shot—but nobody said it was supposed to be. It was silly and fun and full of color and music. That should be enough, as far as they were all concerned.

The next day, Juliet didn't even bother to try to put in a day's work at her office. She conferred with the Methodist Women about the next morning's pancake breakfast, and briefly viewed each of the thirty-five floats—most of which were actually finished—that were scheduled for tomorrow afternoon's parade. She went over, once again, the float order with Reva, and then toured the upstairs of the town hall, where the Crafts and Industry Fair was—more or less—ready to go.

At four, she went back to the ranch and took a long tepid bath and lay down in her undies for forty-five minutes, getting up only after she had fallen asleep and dreamed, disconcertingly, of Cody asking her sadly why she had turned her back on him. She woke with a start, to find two wet tears had run down the sides of her face and into her hair.

She sat up and brushed them away and went to put on her new red dress. When she was ready, she stood before the mirror in her room.

A summer-weight knit, the dress hugged her slim curves to below the waist, where it flared out abruptly. Beneath the flare of the skirt, which fell to midcalf, she wore a red crinoline-edged half-slip. Of course, no one would be seeing the slip, but she did love the naughty way it whispered with each step she took.

Juliet winked at herself in the mirror. She put the leftover sadness from her dream behind her. She was ready for the opening night of the Midsummer Madness Revue.

When the curtain went up, the old Gap Auditorium was *standing room only.* Juliet gave up her own seat to the elderly woman from Ukiah who claimed she'd never missed a first night of the revue in thirty years—but next year, the woman suggested, maybe they'd better arrange to take reservations so the people who really cared could be sure to be accommodated....

Juliet posted herself up near one of the side doors as the house lights went down. Listening to the rustle of excitement in the audience, she couldn't help anticipating the thousand and one things that might go wrong.

But nothing did, excluding a few missed light cues and late entrances, of course. From the first notes of "Sweet Adeline," by the Barbershop Boys, to the closing "Star Spangled Banner," performed by the Gap High Madrigals, it was an evening of pure magic.

All the animals did what their trainers told them to do. Yolanda didn't fool with her bodice once; Juliet even thought she heard one or two sniffles from the audience when the doleful music began at her untimely death. Flat-nosed Jake brought the house down with dramatic renditions of his poems, "Yukon Joe and the Woman He Wronged," and "Show Her Mercy, Not Scorn, She Is Tattered and Torn."

And Cody, wearing a black shirt with mother-of-pearl buttons, black jeans and black boots, had everyone stomping their feet and clapping their hands when he sang the song about the mule. Juliet clapped and stomped with the best of them, singing along at the chorus and applauding wildly at the end.

Since she hadn't heard it in rehearsal, she was not prepared for his second song, which came at the end of the show, right before the patriotic closing number. He wore the same shirt and jeans and sat on a stool in a single spotlight. And he sang about a man who wanted a woman who refused to let herself want him back.

The song was stunningly sensual and yet so sweetly tender at the same time. The audience fell silent—all crackling of programs and crossing of legs ceased. Juliet, who knew she shouldn't, closed her eyes, and let her body relax against the wall at her back.

She allowed herself the forbidden illusion that Cody sang that song for her. And she relived the two wondrous times she'd been in his arms—first, lying across his lap on the front porch of his house, and later, in her office, when he slowly uncovered her breasts, and then made love to them with his mouth.

As the song ended, there was silence. In the hushed moment, Juliet sighed, lost in her fantasy of Cody's lips on her skin.

Then thunderous applause crashed in on her. She snapped upright, darting guilty glances to either side. But no one seemed concerned that she'd just been swooning against the side wall, lost again in taboo moments that she'd sworn to forget. Everyone was riveted to the stage, clapping madly for Cody and his beautiful, seductive song. Juliet, feeling lost and disoriented, pulled herself together and joined in the applause.

Then came "The Star Spangled Banner," and after that, ten minutes' worth of curtain calls. At last, Babe Allen got up and said a few words about the big parade tomorrow and the pancake breakfast—and all the coming attractions over the next ten days.

Juliet went backstage briefly to congratulate everyone on doing a marvelous job, and to fill her own role as director and remind them not to get cocky, since they had nine more performances to go. Her voice broke once while she spoke, because she foolishly made eye contact with Cody, who was staring at her with an unreadable expression on his face, and had a leg hitched up on one of the makeup counters.

When she was through speaking, Cody stood up and invited everyone to McIntyre's for drinks on the house. Juliet stared at him, so achingly handsome in his fancy-buttoned shirt. And she wanted to go—just for a little while.

And why shouldn't she go, after all? The revue was a triumph. She had a right to celebrate.

So she left the auditorium with Jake and Andrea, chattering excitedly with them about the revue and the festival, as they walked the half block to McIntyre's in the romantic light of the gas lamps with a full moon overhead.

The long bar area was packed when they arrived. Every stool was taken, and all the high tables and the high seats round about were full. Juliet jostled her way in with the rest of them, laughing and waving to everyone she knew.

Heady praise filled the close air. "Great job, Juliet!" "Hey, Juliet, way to go!" "We knew you could do it, girl, and we weren't wrong!"

When she got up to the bar, there was a drink—a strawberry daiquiri—plunked right down in front of her, which Cody must have told the bartender she liked. She felt her face warming, wondering if he'd seen her come in, glancing quickly around to find out where he was. But he was nowhere in sight.

She took a long, cool sip. The icy concoction was the best she'd ever had.

Several more people told her how wonderful she was, she received more than one pat on the back and then soon enough another star of the evening appeared at the door, and the crowd turned their approving salutations that way.

Juliet, feeling the beginnings of a happy, hazy glow, leaned back against the bar and tapped her high-heeled shoe to the music from the jukebox in the corner, and decided that tonight made the agony of teaching herself to step forward worthwhile.

She drank the last of the daiquiri, and another appeared at her elbow. When she offered to pay, the bartender waved her money away. She thanked him, took a satisfying sip of the drink and then, weaving through the press of bodies, made her way to the jukebox to scan the selections it offered.

"Choose a few on me, Juliet...." Someone dropped several quarters into her hand. She took her time, sipping her drink, punching up mostly country-western songs about outlaws and hopeless love.

"Having fun?"

The hazy euphoria of the whole evening suddenly seemed to be concentrated in the gray-green eyes of the man who leaned against the side of the jukebox and smiled at her with a sweet kind of fondness, the way he used to before everything changed between them.

She didn't answer. She really felt no pressure to say anything right then. She just indulged in the pleasure of looking at him, and confessing silently that, beyond wanting him, she'd missed him—so very much.

"Are you having fun?" he asked again, his voice gently teasing as it used to be in the old days, when he'd try to lighten her spirits after some little thing would send her into an agony of embarrassment or fright.

She nodded. Down inside her, something shifted.

She understood, at that moment, that some things just had to be allowed to happen. And, though she might suffer in the end, a woman who tried to deny the urgings of her heart would have only lived half a life when it all came down to dust.

She said in a whisper, with no more thought of holding back the truth, "I've missed you."

It was his turn to say nothing. He looked deep in her eyes. At last he answered, "Me, too."

All around them, the party went on. People jostled and joked, loud and excited. But to Juliet, right then, there was no sound but the hard beating of her heart, the quickened rush of her own breath in and out and, far away, the music she'd chosen on the jukebox.

He said what she knew he would say. "Come home with me tonight."

She put her hand on the side of his face, thrilling at the smooth warmth of his freshly shaved skin. He covered her hand with his in an enveloping caress. And then he kissed her palm, his breath like a tender brand on her skin. "I want you, Julie," he said. "I'm tired of trying to pretend I don't."

Her heart took wing.

So what if it couldn't last? So what if it would probably end badly—with her losing a lover, a friend and a client, too? She was thirty years old and had never known the feel of a naked man's body warm and close in the night. The first time ought to be with someone she adored, during the Midsummer Madness Festival, when she was living out her lifelong dream of being the strong, assertive woman she'd always felt was trapped inside her, begging to be set free.

Cody was looking at her, waiting for her answer.

She gave it. "I'm tired of pretending, too, Cody. Yes, I'll go home with you."

Seven

She left her red car in the restaurant's parking lot, and they went home in his pickup, the magical full moon ahead of them all the way, playing hide-and-seek with them through the branches of the trees as they climbed toward the ranch. When they drove through the front gate, the big silvery ball hung suspended, ripe and glorious, heavy on the rim of the far mountains over the north field.

Kemo was waiting, tail wagging and tongue lolling, by the front step. He wriggled over, whining with happiness. Cody scratched him behind the ear and smoothed his sleek black coat before he came around to Juliet's side and flung back the pickup door.

"Come here, woman!" he commanded, and then scooped her up against his chest. Beneath her skirt the red crinoline hem of her slip ballooned up and then settled in a crimson froth over his arm. Juliet laughed and hugged him close.

He bore her up the porch steps and shifted her weight to fiddle with the lock on the big double door. At last the lock turned. He kicked the door open. Then he carried her, both of them laughing, over the threshold, across the foyer to the staircase and up the stairs.

His room was the master bedroom and faced north on the open field. It had a huge bay window, like the one that formed the breakfast nook below, only here there was a curving seat where a person could sit and simply enjoy the view.

Once in the room, the laughter they'd been sharing faded.

Cody set her down before the window and then wrapped his arms around her from behind. For a while they just stood there, with only the silver moon outside for light.

The moment, a suspended place between anticipation and fulfillment, spun out. A thin cloud drifted across the face of the moon, darkening the world in night shadow, and then gently floated by, so that the moon gave full light once more.

"Is this...still what you want?" Cody softly asked in her ear.

She turned in his arms and looked into his face. "Yes."

"Scared?"

"Definitely."

"We'll go slow."

"Good."

She twined her arms around his neck as he lowered his lips to hers. The kiss became a series of kisses, a languorous sensual exploration. His lips brushed her mouth—back and forth, up and down—and then moved on to sweetly caress her chin and her cheeks and the tip of her nose.

He lifted his head after a time and said in a husky voice, "I forgot my manners. Can I get you a drink?"

Juliet, still sweetly hazy from her two daiquiris, shook her head and then lifted her mouth again for more slow, delicious kisses.

Cody willingly obliged her and for a while there were soft sighs and small chuckles in the moonlit bay window overlooking the north field. But soon enough, his hands grew bold. He touched her breasts.

She sighed at that, and arched for him, so that he could caress her to their mutual delight through the fabric of her dress. Then, after a while, he guided her, in slow steps, toward the wide bed, where they both fell back, giggling once again.

When the laughter faded, he rose up on an elbow to look down in her eyes. "Hey, I like this dress," he said.

She gave him a playful, disbelieving frown. "It's not the old me at all."

"I think," he said, tracing a heart on her bare shoulder where he'd just pushed the dress aside, "that I'm beginning to appreciate the *new* you."

"Is that so?"

"Yeah, it's so." His voice was husky now. His hand wandered, down over the sweet rise of her breast and the scooped-out slimness of her belly to the place where the skirt began to flare. He took hold of the skirt there, at her hip, and very slowly began to raise it.

"Juliet Titania Huddleston," he murmured, as the red crinoline-edged slip was revealed, "what have we here?"

She didn't answer, didn't even move, as the skirt was lifted and the red petticoat displayed. When all of it was showing, he gently smoothed its tousled folds, and then kissed her once more. It was a very thorough kiss that ignited her nerve endings and started the familiar meltdown in her abdomen.

"Oh, Cody," she managed to say, shivering a little with excitement—and apprehension—of what was to come.

He whispered something erotic and yet reassuring, as his hand strayed beneath the hem of her skirt until he'd found the elastic waist of the slip. He slid his finger under there—her belly quivered, he whispered "Shh, it's okay"—and then, with slow stroking motions, he stretched the elastic and glided the slip over her hips.

"Lift up, Julie...." He nibbled her ear.

She moaned and raised her hips enough so that he could whisk away the naughty slip. He dropped it then, somewhere on the floor. She certainly didn't notice where, because he was touching her again, his finger slipping beneath the back straps of her high heels, each in turn, sliding them off and away just as he had done with the red slip.

She wore no stockings. He ran a caressing finger up the length of one bare, smooth leg, setting off little heated shivers all along her skin until he reached the place, high on her thigh, where he'd lifted her skirt to get to the red slip.

He boldly went higher, beneath the yards of crimson fabric, till he touched the fragile scrap of cloth that covered the womanly center of her. Never had anyone touched her there before. She gasped and stiffened in awareness. He made more soothing, quieting sounds, and then once again his hand was stroking, petting her through the silky cloth so she forgot everything but the pleasure he gave.

Her body, seeming to know what to do in spite of her inexperience, lifted in invitation beneath his ardent touch. His mouth covered hers again, in an unending kiss, as he rubbed and stroked her and she moved, unashamed, beneath his hand.

Under the flimsy veil of her panties, she grew very wet. She knew he must feel that. For a moment, she froze, embarrassed that he should know such a thing about her body's response to him. But he whispered huskily against her mouth that it was okay, it was just right. Relaxing, allowing herself the freedom once more to revel in this wonder, she began to move again.

He murmured more encouragements, stroking her more swiftly while she writhed and moaned and kissed him with a building sense of urgency that made her clutch his shoulders, inchoately, yearning for a fulfillment that she didn't quite know how to achieve.

But Cody seemed to know. In a smooth, unhurried movement, his hand drifted up her belly. She moaned, not wanting him to stop.

His lips moved over her cheek, to toy with her ear. "It's okay, Julie. Just let yourself go...."

Then his hand was at the elastic of her panties, sliding beneath, moving lower. Juliet gasped, because she knew what he was doing now, just as his hand found her, opened her and began doing what it had done before, only without the thin barrier of cloth. He was caressing the heart of her, in slow, deep, knowing strokes.

It was the most shocking, starkly beautiful thing that had ever happened to her. She gave up all thought of what he must think. She gave up everything to this magic world of the senses, which seemed, behind her closed eyes, to shimmer, like her body, with heat and wonder and building comprehension of the fulfillment to come. Never in her lonely, virginal life, had she known anything half so marvelous as this.

And it kept building, tightening. He went on touching her, his hand moving, it seemed, in instant response to her body's signals as the beautiful sensations coiled tighter and more heated still, second by second, into an erotic infinity that seemed as if it might never, ever end.

And then something happened. Something incredible. From the place he touched her, there was a sudden, unbelievable explosion of sensation. The heart of her bloomed, opening, pulsing, sending ripples of intense feeling outward in an overwhelming release that seared her every nerve and made her throw back her head and cry out loud, a wondrous agony that seemed unending, turned her inside out and left her, at last, limp with satisfaction on the bed.

For the longest time, as the waves of pleasure pulsed and slowly receded, she didn't think. She drifted, boneless, relaxed and content in a way that she had never been before.

Ultimately, though, she began to come back to herself. She gradually became aware that her head was buried against the spread, turned away from him, and that he lay, still fully clothed, against her other side.

As reality reclaimed her, a sudden, distressing thought surfaced. Had she been ridiculous?

She felt her skin flushing as she remembered the way she had writhed and moaned and carried on quite shamelessly, even crying out loud there at the end. She had read in novels that making love could bring great pleasure, but she had never considered what it must look like, to a man, for a woman to thrash and cry out and go a little crazy with the way it felt.

She found, all at once, that she couldn't bear to turn her head to look at him—or even to open her eyes, which were still closed as they'd been since that final ecstasy claimed her.

The silence stretched out. She felt more a fool with each second that passed. She decided, since she wasn't even facing him, that she should at least drum up the nerve to open her eyes. She did, and saw, by the dim light of the moon and stars outside, the fat shape of the pillows at the head of the bed.

One of Cody's arms was beneath her neck, cradling her against his body. And his free hand was still down there, still touching her, still making her body pulse just a little, making her long—oh, this was crazy—to start all over again.

Just as she thought the forbidden thought that she wouldn't mind starting over, his hand moved, leaving the secret heart of her and sliding out from under the rucked-up tangle of her skirt. She quivered a little at the loss of his touch, thinking that her fear must be correct; he must be embarrassed at the way she had behaved, and wondered how he could tactfully get rid of her. She was sure that next he would sit up and pull away from her.

But instead, he touched her face, his fingers scented of her own passion. "Julie? What is it? Are you okay?" His voice, surprisingly, didn't have that distant tone she had expected. With the gentle pressure of his hand, he turned her face to his. "Julie?"

His eyes, in the darkness, shone with what looked like tenderness and concern. She blinked, thinking she saw wrong. But when she opened her eyes again, his expression was the same.

"Is something wrong? Tell me."

She tried to pull away.

He held her steady. "Tell me."

She sighed and relaxed a little. "Oh, Cody...."

"Come on," he coaxed. "Say it."

Bolstered by the appeal in his eyes and reassured by his touch, she managed to tell him. "I guess...I went a little crazy, huh?"

He looked at her for a moment, as what she said sank in. Then he chuckled. "Yeah. Yeah, you sure did."

"I...made a fool of myself. I know it." She moved to sit up.

He gently pulled her down and canted up on an elbow to lean over her. "Not so fast, there." His eyes were full of understanding. "I said you went crazy. I didn't say anything about your making a fool of yourself."

"But I—"

"You were beautiful. Sexy. Incredible."

"Oh, Cody...."

"I was so turned on, I couldn't think straight." He pushed his hips against her a little more tightly. "As a matter of fact, I still am...."

"What?"

"Turned on."

She felt what he meant as he pressed close against her. "Oh." She dared a small smile. "You were? You are?"

"You bet."

"Then you still want to, um..."

"More than anything." He kissed her nose.

She realized she believed him. Relief and happiness flooded her; her whole body went lax. She wrapped her arms around him and kissed him, full on the mouth, with all the warmth and excitement she herself was feeling right then.

When the kiss was done she thought of something else that needed to be considered, and pulled back to ask, "Cody?"

"Yeah?" He rolled away enough that he no longer pinned her to the bed, and she took the opportunity to sit up and gather her feet under her dress.

"Well, um..." She found it difficult to go on. He looked at her, waiting. She hesitated for a moment more, not knowing exactly how to broach the subject, but then she sucked in a breath and plunged in. "I didn't bring anything. For contraception."

"Don't worry." In a lithe movement, he sat up and left the bed, crossing to a dresser where he opened a drawer and pulled out a small pouch that she realized must contain a condom.

She blushed, glad that the issue was settled. "Good."

Then neither of them did anything for a moment. They just looked at each other, and they were both smiling. At that moment it occurred to Juliet that the shattering completion he'd already brought her to had made what was to come seem less frightening.

She held out a hand to him. He came back to the bed and took it, giving it a warm, companionable squeeze. Then he let go, set the small pouch on the bedstand and sat down. The bed gave slightly beneath his weight. He pulled off his black boots, one at a time.

Juliet, still seated Indian-style behind him, watched the simple actions with joy and a kind of awe. At last, after years of watching and wondering from the sidelines, she would discover the secrets of the ultimate mystery between men and women. And she'd learn them with Cody, the most beautiful man in the entire world.

Cody slipped off his socks. And then she saw his arms move as he unsnapped his shirt. The marvelous symmetry of his back came into view as the shirt was removed and tossed over a chair. Then he stood, and he unbuttoned his jeans and took them off, too. And finally he got rid of his briefs, sliding them off casually, without fanfare, the action as natural as dropping to the bed and pulling off his boots had been.

She had never seen a completely naked man except in pictures. His body, she thought, was like a sculpture, almost too perfect and beautiful to be real flesh and blood. He was still aroused.

She moistened her lips a little in nervousness, wondering if he would fit inside her. And then she told herself not to be silly, of course he would fit. He was a man and she was a woman, and they were made to fit.

He came to her, taking the few steps back to the bed, and reached for her hand. She gave it, without hesitating, and he pulled her up to her knees on the edge of the bed. Then he found the hem of her dress and he tugged it up, over her head. She raised her arms and felt it glide along her skin, beyond her lifted fingertips and away. Her fine, straight hair flowed with it, and then drifted back down to settle lightly around her shoulders.

He looked at her, in the red lacy bra and matching panties. So tenderly, he said, "Aw, Julie. Naughty girl."

She told him pertly, "Red's my color now."

He said, "It suits you, now," and reached for her. She held out her arms, and twined them around his neck. Their bodies met, there at the edge of the bed.

His thighs felt strong and hard against the supple smoothness of hers, and the crisp hair on his chest rubbed the soft swells of her breasts above her bra. He bent his head and kissed her, and Juliet lifted her mouth to him, eager for the taste of his lips.

The kiss was long and audaciously carnal. Juliet gloried in it, her hands avidly stroking his back and the strong cords of muscle at his neck, then toying in the silky hair at his nape. She brazenly rubbed her whole body against him, pleasured not only at the feel of him, but at his response to her, which was clear in the low sounds he made in his throat, the hungry way his lips took hers and the jutting evidence of his excitement that pushed against her at the place where their thighs joined.

After a time, he began kissing her throat, which she obligingly arched for him. His lips trailed down to her breasts. He kissed each one through its shield of lace, and then he unhooked the front clasp and slipped the bra off and away.

He began kissing her breasts, as he had done that afternoon in her office, teasing them at first with light nibbles and licks, and then more thoroughly, sucking and cupping them with his hands. Juliet, lost in that marvelous realm of the senses he so expertly created, fell back on the bed; Cody followed her down.

His mouth worked magic at her breast, while his hand trailed down her quivering belly to disappear once again beneath the elastic waistband of her panties. She moaned and bucked in excitement as he began, again, to bring her to readiness, pausing only long enough to slide the wisp of silk off and out of the way.

Now they were both totally nude. His hand continued to stroke and arouse her, and Juliet felt the build to climax begin once again. Though a part of her longed to just ride the crest of the wave of pleasure he created to its own fulfillment, she grabbed his wrist and stilled his hand.

He froze and opened his eyes to look at her.

"If you keep going, I'll finish without you," she managed on a gasping breath.

"That's okay."

"No," she told him. "I want…everything, Cody. I want you. Please?"

Shyly, both curious and hesitant at the same time, she reached for him, encircled his hardness. He gasped, and his hand retreated from the heart of her just a little, so that it only rested on her soft mound. She smiled, and stroked him experimentally, and he groaned and lifted his hips. Juliet thought it absolutely marvelous, to see him gasp and move in response to her touch, just as she had moved when he touched her.

"If you keep that up," he warned in a low growl, "*I'll* be the one finishing without *you.*"

She kissed him then and pulled away to find the small pouch on the nightstand. Blushing a little, she asked to be allowed to help put it on. He obliged her, showing her what to do, groaning again when she slipped it over him, and guided it in place.

Then, when it was on, his hand found her again, and he stroked her some more, making sure she was as ready as she could be, given this was her first time.

At last, he moved above her and gently nudged her thighs apart. He positioned himself and, very gently, lowered his weight until she began to feel the pressure of him, pushing to breach the barrier her body held out against his male invasion.

She made a small sound of discomfort. He swore that after this time, it would never hurt again. And his voice was so tender and full of concern that she knew he would have trouble at the prospect that he would have to hurt her now.

So, bold as the woman she was becoming, and so swiftly he didn't know what she planned, she wrapped her legs around him and thrust herself against him, breaking the barrier herself.

It hurt. A burning, scraping kind of pain. And Cody cried out her name as he filled her, sounding like it hurt him, too.

And then he stayed very still, stretching her to the limit, so that she could absorb and adjust to his presence there. In the stillness her own breath came in hard little pants. And she concentrated on it, commanding it to slow, telling her body to relax, the worst was over.

And, incredibly, her body believed her. She felt her inner muscles slackening their frantic hold on him. The pain receded, and she began to realize how complete and good it felt, to be with him in this most intimate of ways, to be connected, to be filled.

It felt . . . why, it felt . . . exciting. And yet satisfying, too, to have his big body covering hers, and him deep within her. It felt as if . . . as if she was becoming aroused again. She moaned.

And he seemed to sense, as if the male in him knew this, that her moan was no longer one of discomfort, but of building excitement. Slowly he lifted his hips. Juliet moaned again. And he came down to fill her once more.

"You're okay?" he breathed against her cheek.

"Yes." She clutched his back and lifted her body to meet his next thrust. "Yes, Cody, yes. . . ."

He said, "I'll try to be careful. . . ." His voice was strained with his effort to hold back, to go slow for her sake.

She felt the urgency, the tension in him, as he tried to wait for her, to give her time to reach the end with him. But it was no use, not this first time, and she knew it. To have him inside her, she had found, was a delicious thing. And that was enough to discover for right now.

So she boldly pushed her hips against him, urging him to lose himself the way she had earlier. He moaned, muttered roughly, "Don't. . . ."

And then he surrendered to his own need, moving hard and fast within her, and at last thrusting a final, deep lunge. She clung to him, holding him fast inside, as his completion came.

When it was over, she cradled him close, feeling his heartbeat slow, and his breath come less frantically into his chest. She stroked his back, marveling at the hollows and hard muscles there.

At last he stirred, lifting up on his arms and gazing down into her flushed face. "I meant to wait for you."

"It was beautiful, just the way it was."

He smiled then, that right-sided smile that, lately, seemed to steal her breath. And she pulled him back down, so she could feel him all along the length of her.

She whispered fiercely in his ear, "Oh, Cody. Thank you. I was beginning to think I'd never know...about the things that can happen between a man and a woman."

He lifted up enough to give her a rueful smile. "This isn't going to be like the last time you thanked me, is it? When the next thing you said was to stay away from you?"

Juliet pulled him back down. "No way.... Stay as close to me as you want to. The closer the better." She hugged him tight.

Cody hugged her in return. For a while, they just held each other. Then he lifted up and kissed her sweetly on each cheek, taking a languorous time to comb her hair with gentle fingers into a fan around her face. Then, reluctantly, he pulled away and got up to visit the bathroom.

When he was gone, Juliet lay there unashamed, nude upon the bed. From outside, faintly, came the crow of a rooster. Juliet smiled at the dim ceiling overhead. Black Bart. At it again.

Some moments, she thought, as she lay there waiting for Cody to return, were too beautiful to bear. Like this moment, right now, in Cody's moonlit bedroom, sprawled across the rumpled spread which, she knew, now bore evidence that she was no longer a virgin. It was a moment of pure happiness.

Outside, Black Bart crowed again. Juliet rolled her head to look out the window. She couldn't see the moon. Sometime while she and Cody made love, it must have gone down. The stars now held sway, a million pinpoints of light poked in the ebony fabric of the sky.

It was at that precise moment, as she gazed at the star-scattered sky, that the truth hit her. It came at her with all the flattening force of a runaway train, so fast and over-whelming that she had no time to throw up her usual defenses.

She, Juliet Huddleston, who should have known better, had gone and fallen in love with Cody McIntyre!

It was like drowning, in a way, to finally admit it, this truth she'd been running from for over two weeks now. Like water, it flowed over her, and she was buoyed by it, at the same time as she felt it closing over her head, taking her air.

I love Cody McIntyre....

Stunned, Juliet lay there. How had it happened?

The answer came: she'd let it happen. By indulging in her fantasies about him, by surrendering to her own desire and coming here to his bed tonight.

Oh, it was not a bright thing to have done. It did not fit in with her plans for herself in the least.

But, nonetheless, it was true. She loved Cody.

The door to the adjoining bath squeaked. Startled, Juliet sat up with a gasp. She looked across the room at Cody, who stood silhouetted in the light he'd turned on behind him.

He must have seen some of her stunned confusion in her face. "Julie? You all right?"

She forced her mouth to smile. "Yes, Cody. I'm fine." He switched off the light and came to her, across the smooth wooden floor.

She kept smiling as he approached. In her mind, her own voice whispered, *I love you. I love you, Cody.*

But she did not say the words out loud. She just couldn't tell him. Not now. Perhaps not ever.

She had to be realistic. Cody was not the man for her—not in the long run. He was way out of her league. Oh, she'd learned to assert herself a little, and she was wearing brighter clothes. But deep inside, the shy mouse still quivered. And Cody was and always would be Gap High's star quarterback, a compassionate hunk who made every woman weak in the knees with just a glance. If he ever found the right woman for him, she'd be his equal, someone as gorgeous and outgoing as Cody himself.

And if Juliet had a smidgen of sense left, she would do her best not to even let herself imagine what it might be like to spend the rest of her days at his side. Because it would never happen, not in real life. This beauty and magic was all a big fantasy. Midsummer Madness, that was all.

Cody knelt before her on the bed. "Julie?" His tender fingers smoothed a strand of hair behind her ear. "What is it? Tell me."

"It's nothing." She gave the lie sweetly. "Really." She swayed toward him, lifting her mouth. He kissed her, and she sighed against him, pulling him close. A wave of sadness washed over her—and then flowed away.

Her love was her secret. She'd learn to accept that. And she'd make the most of every moment they had. This was Midsummer Madness. Brief, crazy and sweet. Her time to know ecstasy, and her time to shine in the light.

Eight

It took Cody a few days before he began to suspect that Juliet was shutting him out.

At first, nothing could bother him. He was as content as a cat in a creamery. He even got himself involved up to his eyeballs in Midsummer Madness—and then discovered that he didn't mind a bit. In fact, he was so conspicuously available that Andrea Oakleaf, with a gleam in her gunmetal-gray eyes, declared that she greatly admired his sudden awakening to civic responsibility.

Thus, he was tied into an apron at the Methodist Women's Pancake Breakfast. He performed the humble task of dishwasher because Yardley Forbes, brought down by an excess of celebration the night before, didn't show up.

At the parade, when they were one judge short, he was prevailed upon to fill in, and marked his choices on the ballots for most clever, most original, most beautiful, most just about everything else a man could possibly imagine. There were over thirty floats, and Cody was reasonably sure there were at least that many categories. Not surprisingly, just about every entrant walked away with "best of" something or other.

At the frog jump on Sunday, somehow he ended up down on his knees at the finish line, trying to fairly determine which little croaker crossed the line first. That night, after the revue, when he and Julie were at last alone, he complained that refereeing the finish line for racing frogs was not a dignified assignment for a man.

She laughed, kissed him and told him that it took a real man to get down in the dirt at frog level, the way he had, and still look commanding and authoritative when he stood up. When he frowned at her doubtfully, she kissed him again and thanked him quite sweetly, and he realized that he'd probably get down in the dirt again the moment she asked him.

He was enchanted. And with Julie Huddleston, of all people. It was as if all these years he'd been looking at her through some hazy obstruction, like one of the lace curtains that used to hang in the bay window of his parents' bedroom before it became his room and he had it made over to suit himself.

Somehow, over the past few weeks, the lace curtain that had obscured her had been slowly pulled aside and he saw her clearly, slim and lovely, wearing a red dress and smiling that sweet, innocent smile that could turn naughty and tempting the minute they were alone.

It astounded him, took his breath away, the way she could be when they were alone. Hers was a mesmerizing combination of innocence, frank curiosity and natural sensuality that got him so turned on, he often found it difficult to hold out long enough to see that she found her full pleasure every time they made love.

More than once, it ended like the first time, with him hitting the peak before she got there. But she never minded. She'd stroke his back and hold him and get him going all over again. And the second time, he'd make sure he drove her wild before surrendering to his own satisfaction.

Never before had it been like this for him with a woman. Never so fun. Never so exciting. Never so tender. And never so comfortable.

If he had been a man prone to self-analysis, he might have decided that his looks had always, in the ways that mattered, kept people at a distance. Women, especially, behaved toward him as if he wasn't a real human being with the same needs and desires as all people had. Too many women had treated him as if he were a *thing,* designed for their pleasure, to swoon and ooh and ah over. A sex object, not a man.

That had been fine while he was very young, when his wants had been simpler—a few drinks, a few laughs and, later, a purely physical release. But as the years passed, it had simply not been enough. He'd retreated from encounters that didn't satisfy him any longer.

And maybe, he began to suspect, he'd retreated from his friends and community, as well. He'd become, as Andrea Oakleaf had so astringently pointed out, unwilling to commit himself on any level—from accepting a date with yet another woman who would swoon over him and not treat him as an equal, to getting up on stage every evening and doing his bit for his town in the Midsummer Madness Revue.

But now, at last, with Julie, all that seemed to have changed. He wanted to spend every night with her, just like it was now, making love until both of them were grinning with satisfaction. And then they would drift off to sleep together, with her cradled in the crook of his arm, her hair laid across his shoulder like strands of the finest pale gold silk. With her beside him, he didn't mind at all committing himself to do whatever had to be done when it came to the festival.

They'd been friends forever, in that distant way, and both of them had known that he had done most of the giving in the past; he had taken care of her and looked out for her over the years. But now, from the night she gave her innocence to him, everything seemed, to Cody, to have turned around the other way. Now she gave. Of her laughter and her warmth and her gentleness that he hadn't known he needed till it was there in her touch and in her hazel eyes.

As the days of Midsummer Madness came and went, he longed to tell her all of this, to share in words all the ways his life was better since they had become more than friends. But therein lay the only cloud on this current chain of sunbright days.

As the days passed, he began to notice that every time he tried to talk to her about what was happening between them, she deftly changed the subject. She would just *have* to ask his opinion about some minor detail concerning the festival, or she'd suddenly remember some important thing she just couldn't put off doing for another moment.

For the first few days, Cody accepted with good grace her skittishness when it came to talking about the two of them. Truth to tell, he himself had little experience in talking about the future with a woman. But by midweek, it had begun to nag at him.

After all, he just wanted to talk about it; he himself wasn't sure what it all meant yet. But she wouldn't talk about it. No matter how innocent-seeming her tactics she wouldn't even let him broach the subject without suddenly shutting him out.

He decided to try a little harder to get through to her. He thought maybe if he could get her away from everything for a while, somewhere where there were no distractions, that he might get her to open up about her feelings when it came to the two of them.

So on Wednesday, in spite of his work and her work and all the demands of the festival, he convinced her to play hooky from everything until noon, under the pretext of giving her her first riding lesson.

He tacked up Lucky, a twelve-year-old sorrel gelding and the gentlest of his three horses, for her, going through the whole process very slowly, from bridle to saddle cinch, demonstrating it all so that next time she could try it herself. Then he explained that Lucky liked it best if she mounted from the left and got down on the right.

He held the reins while she stuck her left foot in the stirrup. She then made a reasonably good show of swinging her right foot over and seating herself.

To start, he led Lucky around the paddock a few times, allowing horse and rider to get used to things. Finally he let Julie hold the reins herself and she cautiously ambled around the enclosed space while he reminded her to keep Lucky's head down. After a while, she made it up to a fairly credible canter, though he saw a lot of daylight between her cute little bottom and the saddle. He suggested, more than once, that she get into Lucky's rhythm, or she was going to be sorry later.

At last, he mounted his own favorite, Blaze, and, with Kemo bouncing alongside, they left the paddock, crossed the north field and entered the trees at the west corner. This was the beginning of what in his family had always been known as the Sunset Trail.

The Sunset Trail was good for a beginner because it meandered lazily up the side of Sunset Mountain, never getting too narrow or too steep. Most of the way, Sunset Creek bubbled along below the trail, tumbling cheerfully over the rocks and providing shaded views of clear water, white-barked birch trees and lichen-covered boulders.

Cody, sure of Lucky's tractableness but playing it safe anyway, rode ahead, keeping it to a walk. Kemo raced up and down the hillside, barking occasionally at invisible lizards and such, but staying clear of the horses' hooves.

The ride was uneventful and pleasant, just as Cody had intended. Squirrels scolded the rambunctious dog from the trees, jays squawked and the morning sun fell in glittering, shifting patterns through the lacework of the pine branches overhead.

Soon enough, they reached the spot he had sought, where the trail dipped down to the side of the creek. There, the creek widened out to a pool, and the space the pool made between the trees gave a few patches of toasty sun for basking in.

He dismounted and helped Julie down. Kemo, who was still bouncing distractingly around, was granted a stern glance. The dog whined and dropped to the ground to lie panting happily in the sun.

Cody had brought a blanket, which he spread at the base of a boulder. There, he and Julie sat down, their backs against the big rock. Once comfortable, they shared a few moments of companionable silence while the horses drank from the creek and nibbled the short grass nearby.

Eventually, Julie sighed. "This is heaven, Cody. My fantasy-come-true."

He remembered that night she'd spoken before the association, when he gave her a ride home because that outrageous car of hers wouldn't start. She'd said that living at his ranch was "not quite so permanent as a dream. More temporary. Like a fantasy." He decided that it was time, now

that he'd gotten them off to themselves, to pursue the subject that had been on his mind so much lately.

He asked, "So is that what this is to you, a fantasy?"

She turned those wide hazel eyes on him. "What do you
mean, Cody?"

"You and me. Are we just a fantasy?"

She tipped her head, as if the idea demanded great
thought. But when she spoke, it was not to answer. "You
sound disapproving."

"I just want to know."

"What?" She looked innocent.

He tried again. "You and me. Are we just a fantasy?"

She smiled. "Oh, Cody. What makes you ask that?"

"Look. Just answer me."

She leaned toward him. "Yes, we're a fantasy. A fantasy
come true."

"What exactly does that mean?"

"Oh, Cody...." She kissed his neck, her soft lips brushing his skin.

"Julie...." The point of the discussion began to elude
him.

She whispered, "We're the most wonderful thing that's
ever happened to me."

The scent of her surrounded him. It was clean and fresh
like soap and water, but with just a hint of a citrusy something that added a provocative tartness.

"Julie...."

He had thought that this would be a perfect spot for
talking. But now, with the soft caress of her lips on his skin,
it occurred to him that more than talking could easily go on
here. They would not be disturbed. Without fearing inter-
ruption, he might take off the cropped red knit shirt she was
wearing and kiss her breasts. He might caress her in the
sunlight, freely, to their mutual delight.

He valiantly tried to forge on. "I want to talk about where this is going, that's all."

She nibbled his ear. "Fine. If you want to."

"Julie, I'm serious...."

She trailed a finger down the front of his white T-shirt and did what, just yesterday, he had told her aroused him no end: she cupped his manhood through his jeans. "I'm listening."

But by then whether or not she was listening didn't matter in the least. Cody's good sense had lost out to his senses. He buried his hands in her hair and pulled her face up to his. His lips covered hers, and she eagerly murmured, "Oh, Cody, oh yes...."

He wasted no time in making his imaginings real. He lifted the hem of her little shirt and tugged it over her head, tossing it away to where it caught on a willow branch. Next, he took her bra away. And then, his eyes heavy with building desire, he looked at her, in the sunlight, at her small, high breasts and her shell-pink nipples that were already standing up, eager for his touch. He took one in his mouth, glorying in her moan of pleasure, and guided her down on the blanket, working at the buttons of her jeans as he suckled her. She helped him, moaning, eager as he was, somehow managing to toe off her boots and shimmy out of her jeans and shuck her panties in mere minutes, while he went on kissing her breasts.

It was crazy, what she did to him, what none of the series of skilled lovers he'd known before had ever done. She made him forget everything, except her sweet face and hazel eyes. She made him forget his own intentions to get a little clarity between them.

Lord, he was starved for her, as if they hadn't made love mere hours ago. She wriggled and moaned and brushed him with her soft hand through the rough cloth of his jeans. He touched her, and she was ready.

He couldn't wait. Didn't want to wait. And if her hungry moans and thrusting hips meant anything, neither did she.

He ripped down his zipper, and got his pants out of the way and slid on one of the condoms that, lately, he had sense enough to carry everywhere they went. Then he rose over her. She opened for him, her face flushed, her eyes closed. He looked down at her, astounded that he could ever have thought her plain.

"Julie..." It was a rough, raspy sound, something that felt torn from the deepest part of him, that part that only she had touched—at last, after a long string of lonely years.

She reached for him, her slim arms pulling him down. He entered her, sliding in easily, encountering no resistance, only heat and eagerness and a long sigh of welcome. She moved beneath him, urging him to lose himself.

And he thought again, in an unformed, clouded way, of the aim he'd had in coming here, and the way she had averted it. Somewhere, in the heart of his desire and excitement, a tiny kernel of anger formed.

It was hardly conscious; he really didn't even acknowledge the feeling. But he was hurt, because he had begun to fear that she thought of him as all the others had: as an object, a handsome face whose heart didn't matter, someone to spin fantasies around, but not someone with whom the future needed to be discussed.

The unrecognized anger strengthened him, so that the maelstrom of pleasure didn't suck him down. He held out against her sweet urging, long enough to bring her to a shattering release, her head flung back, soft neck straining, to watch her lose herself completely, twisting and moaning beneath him, calling out his name.

At last, when she went limp and satisfied, he came down full length upon her. She clutched him, melting against him, murmuring little wordless things, her breath warm against his ear. The moment was unbearably sweet, and his own desire mounted again within it, stimulated beyond holding back now, by the totality of her surrender.

He began to move. She sighed in pleasure, replete but still so willing, and moved in rhythm with him. The rhythm mounted, took on a life of its own, and Cody, at the center of it, surrendered to it utterly. The rapturous pressure built, until it could no longer be contained, and then it claimed him, splintering outward in a hot burst of pulsing sensation. He thrust deeply into her; she rose to meet him. And he called out, flinging his head back, crying his completion to the sun-dazzled sky.

After a time when there was only her soft body beneath his and her gently stroking hands, he lifted up, kissed the tip of her nose and then rolled away to dispose of the condom and straighten his clothes. It was quickly done, and left him time to turn and watch her as she reclaimed her tossed-away top and bra, put them on and then wriggled into her jeans and pulled on her boots.

She glanced at him now and then as she dressed herself, sending him a grin or a sweet, conspiratorial wink. At first, he simply enjoyed watching her, feeling close and companionable after the overwhelming wonder of the intimacy they had just shared.

But then he remembered his original purpose in riding out here. He frowned, wondering if he really wanted to try to get through to her again. She was now sitting beside him, fully dressed, working the tangles from her pale, fine hair with a little pocket comb she'd carried in her jeans.

Maybe he should just let it be, he thought. The ride to get here had been a pleasure, their lovemaking beautiful. Why spoil the morning with talk about a subject she seemed not to want him to broach?

In the silence of his indecision, one of the horses whickered softly and nipped the other one. Cody asked, "Julie?"

She glanced at him, her comb paused in midstroke, "Hmm?"

He boldly tried again, "I still want to talk."

"About what?"

"About you and me, about this whole thing between us...."

Suddenly she was pocketing her comb and glancing at her watch. "Oh my goodness, it's past eleven. I have to meet Babe Allen for lunch at twelve-thirty. Can you believe it? She's thinking of donating six Hummel figurines from the Gift Emporium for the raffle tomorrow evening."

Cody stared at her. "What's a Hummel?"

She stood up. "You know. Those china figurines. They're collector's items."

He looked up at her, irritation tightening his stomach. He'd mentioned the two of them, and suddenly she couldn't sit still a second longer. "So?" His voice was somewhat curt. "You have to have lunch with Babe to get her figurines for the raffle?"

"More or less." She glanced away modestly. "Babe wants to talk about next year, and whether I'll be directing things again."

She began motioning him to get up, so she could shake out the blanket. "I just didn't realize how late it was getting."

"Julie, wait." He seized her arm when she knelt to grab the blanket's hem.

"Don't." She jerked away, rocking back on her heels—and then immediately looked ashamed. "I'm sorry. I really am. I just didn't know how late it was getting.... Now, can you please get up?"

For a long minute, he stared at her. Finally he said, "You can't get away from this forever. Sometime we have to talk about you and me."

Suddenly she looked like she might cry. "I know."

He felt like a rat, bringing tears to her eyes like that, but this was important, so he forged on. "Then when?"

She was still kneeling, though she'd forgotten all about shaking out the blanket. She seemed, all at once, to realize that he wasn't going to get up until she gave him an answer. So she stood, a somewhat frantic move, and hurried to the edge of the creek. She looked down, perhaps at her own blurred reflection in the slowed waters of the little pool.

Then, abruptly, she turned to him. "Are you... Do you like this? I mean, are you enjoying what's happening between you and me?" Her voice was soft, hesitant, reminiscent of the old Julie, who was so little in evidence of late.

"Hell, yes."

"Then what... what's wrong?"

He felt more like a rat by the second. "I didn't say anything was wrong, exactly."

"Then why can't we just... enjoy this?"

"We are. I am. That isn't the point. I want to talk, that's all."

She looked at him, her expression desperate and unhappy. Finally she pleaded, "Can't we just wait? Please?"

"Until when?"

She sighed. "Until the festival's over. Can't we just have a wonderful time until then?"

"Live out your fantasy, you mean?" His voice had a bitter edge.

She looked away. "Yes. I suppose."

He was quiet, considering, thinking grimly that the only reason she could be putting him off was because she saw no future for them. He was her fantasy-come-true and nothing more. Soon enough, she'd be ready for reality again—and he'd be out the door.

He forced himself to weigh her proposal, trying to be philosophical instead of giving in to his hurt and his anger that she would use him this way. Once he considered it, he realized that he fully intended to do just as she asked. He wanted the next few days, too. And maybe, when they finally talked, it wouldn't turn out as bad as he feared.

He agreed to her terms with a casual shrug that belied the sudden heaviness of his heart. "All right. Until the festival's over. Sunday night, after the last performance of the revue. Then we'll talk about you and me."

All of a sudden, she was smiling, holding out her hand. "Good. Now, come on. I really do have to get back."

He stood up, feeling an answering smile tug on his own lips as Kemo also rose and stretched and whined eagerly to be on the way. Her slender hand closed around his. She pulled him close and wrapped her arms around him, lifting her mouth.

She kissed him—a sweet, playful kiss. And then she was spinning away from him, grabbing up the blanket, shaking it out. He watched her, thinking ruefully that it was hard to stay mad at her when she was so damned adorable, so full of laughter and vitality, her pink skin still glowing from their lovemaking, her hazel eyes alight.

Hell, maybe she *was* using him. But it was almost worth it to see her this way—timid Julie Huddleston, taking on the world at last.

He resolved to do it her way, to enjoy the waning days of Midsummer Madness at her side, and not to think of what would happen when the festival drew to a close, when she would finally have to reveal to him the secrets she would not share now.

"Help me fold this thing," she begged sweetly.

He went to her, smiling, his resolve lightening his mood. Right then, he honestly thought everything would be fine until Sunday night.

In his own way, Cody McIntyre was as innocent as Juliet when it came to the ways of the heart.

Nine

Babe was waiting patiently in the sandwich shop, sipping an iced tea, when Juliet slid into the seat across from her.

"I'm sorry, Babe." Juliet glanced at the time, which she'd been doing, harriedly, through the entire drive from the ranch.

Babe waved her hand. "It's okay. I had a cool drink to keep me company."

"Cody took me riding." Juliet delicately shifted in her seat. "My first time. I think tomorrow I'll be feeling what a good time I had."

Babe grinned. "You and Cody are quite an item." Juliet felt her face pinkening, hated that it was happening, and knew that it was pinkening all the more. "A lot of women in this town are green with envy, I'll tell you."

Juliet, who didn't want to think about how much other women wanted Cody, grabbed for the menu. "Well," she asked overbrightly, "have you already ordered?"

Babe, who was there with the firm intention of getting Juliet's commitment to run Midsummer Madness next year, knew when a subject would gain her no points. "No, I waited for you." She also whipped open her menu and studied it with great interest. "The waitress said the pastrami is fresh, but she recommends the grilled turkey and Swiss...."

Juliet relaxed as she realized Babe would not pursue the subject of herself and Cody any further. The waitress came and took their order.

The meal was a success in the eyes of both women. Not only was the grilled turkey and Swiss as good as the waitress had promised, but Juliet got her figurines for the raffle the following evening. Babe, for her part, extracted from Juliet a commitment that she'd handle the festival next year. Babe also insisted on picking up the check.

When she left the restaurant, Juliet felt so good that she wanted to share it all with Cody. Babe had even sworn she could get the association to raise Juliet's fee. The money, next year, would go toward the new seats that were needed in the Gap Auditorium.

Deciding that she just had to tell Cody all about it right now, Juliet strolled the few blocks to McIntyre's. She was sure that he'd still be there, finishing up after the lunch rush.

She pushed back the door and strode into the cool dimness, blinded for the briefest moment as her eyes adjusted after the bright sunlight outside. When the long bar came into focus, the first thing she saw was Cody—and a beautiful woman.

He stood with his back to the door. The woman, a tall redhead in a silky blouse and slim skirt, was bending close to him, lifting an unlit cigarette to her lips.

Cody picked up a pack of bar matches and gave her a light. Then he murmured something brief and immediately moved away. The woman caught his arm. Cody looked down at her red-nailed hand, and then very deliberately back into her face. She let go.

Juliet understood that the scene she was witnessing happened several times a week. Cody was an incredibly handsome man, and his business brought him into contact with available women every day. He was bound to get offers. She herself had seen him get offers all the time over the years.

But this time, the sight of him smoothly turning down another lovely woman twisted inside her like the turning of a sharp knife. She wanted to whirl and run.

But he'd already seen her. "Julie!" His voice was full of pleasure at the sight of her. Even Juliet, in the agony of her insecurity, could hear that.

Behind him, the beautiful redhead gave Juliet a long, cold glance. The woman was probably wondering what a man like Cody could see in someone like Juliet Huddleston.

Cody strode across the oak floor, his eyes alight. Juliet, accepting a chaste hug and a quick, welcoming kiss, asked, "Who is that?"

Cody followed the direction of her gaze, saw the redhead, and shrugged. "I think she said her name was Laura. New in town. An agent for Bruckner's Real Estate."

"She's . . . very pretty."

"Yeah," Cody agreed with another shrug that said the subject of the redhead wasn't one that had much interest for him. He put his arm around her shoulders, "Come on, let's go to the office." He led her out of the bar, asking before they'd even made it through the kitchen, "So how'd it go with Babe? I know you're dying to tell me." He grinned his right-sided grin.

As she gazed up at him, Juliet forgot all about the beautiful woman with the fiery hair. There was nothing else in the world but her love for him, so strong right then that she had to press her lips together to keep from blurting out, *I love you, Cody,* while they were walking through the kitchen, with cooks and pot washers all over the place.

It had been that way this morning, when he kept trying to get her to talk about the two of them. She'd suspected what he wanted to tell her—that she shouldn't get too attached to him, because what they had couldn't last forever. She'd longed to throw herself at him, passionately declare her never-ending love and beg him not to leave her. But she hadn't, because she didn't want to lose him any sooner than it was going to happen anyway.

So instead of speaking honestly, she'd shamelessly seduced him. And then later, when he tried to talk again, she'd pretended to be in a big hurry to meet with Babe. In the end, he'd agreed to wait until Sunday night to have their discussion about the future.

And she was grateful. She was determined to keep her mouth shut about her hopeless love and enjoy the few days they had left.

"Julie?" He was looking into her eyes, his expression concerned. "What is it? Suddenly you look a million miles away."

"I'm sorry. Just thinking."

"About what?"

"Oh, everything...." She gestured vaguely as he followed her into his office and closed the door.

"About Babe, you mean?"

"Yes. Yes, about Babe. She's donating the figurines, and that's not all...."

The few precious remaining days of Midsummer Madness passed much too quickly. It seemed to Juliet that she merely blinked, and it was already Saturday, the next-to-last day of the festival. That night there would be no revue—because there was the Gold Rush Ball instead.

Juliet's entire day was spent at the Oddfellows Hall over on North Pine Street, supervising the decorating crew and helping the musicians—a six-piece band, including washboard and fiddle, all friends of Flat-nosed Jake's—to set up. Cody was in and out all day, lending a hand wherever he could. He urged Juliet to come over to the restaurant for a quick dinner at five-thirty, but she simply couldn't spare the time. At six, she rushed home, grabbed a sandwich, showered and got into her costume.

At seven, she was looking herself over in the full-length mirror on the back of her bedroom door. She wore a navy blue mid-nineteenth century soldier's uniform, complete with shiny brass buttons, black boots and a billed hat. She saluted her reflection, deciding she presented a fair representation of Lotta Crabtree in one of her most beloved impersonations, The Drummer Boy. She'd even managed to borrow a drum and drumsticks from the elementary school.

The costume, which she'd decided on after long deliberation, had not been easy to come by. On Thursday morning, she'd ended up making a special trip to a shop in Sacramento to find it. And she was paying quite a bit for it—mostly because she'd had such time restraints that she'd been forced to get it early and wouldn't be returning it until Monday, when the festival was over.

When the festival was over....

The drummer boy in the mirror looked back at her through sad hazel eyes.

Juliet shook herself and turned away from her own mournful reflection. Her magical week had been everything she could have dreamed of—and it wasn't over yet.

She drove back to town in her red car, with the windows down and the radio up high to keep her spirits from sagging. Actually, having the radio on loud served another purpose. It kept the engine's irritating knocking noise from bothering her. She reminded herself—again—that she'd have to get that looked into, just as soon as the festival was over.

As soon as the festival was over....

The thought, again, made her sad. She cranked the radio up another notch and stoutheartedly sang along.

Before going to the hall, she stopped in at her own office. From her safe, she collected the cashboxes that would be used that night, as well as the rolls of tickets that Jake had had printed a week ago and given her to hold until the ball. At seven-thirty, she reached the Oddfellows Hall. She was in luck and didn't have to park in back because someone pulled out just as she drove up. She got one of the six spaces right on the street in front of the hall.

Leaving her drum and sticks in the car to collect later, Juliet scooped up the rolls of tickets and the two cashboxes and made for the double front door.

Inside, the brick building was comfortably cool, as well as rather grand by Emerald Gap standards. The lobby area was graced by a crystal chandelier donated in the twenties by Evan McMulch, patriarch of the McMulch family. The McMulches had once owned the now-closed Royale mine and they still ran McMulch's Lumberyard, for which Juliet kept the books.

The walls of the lobby, serendipitously for the Gold Rush Ball, boasted a series of murals depicting the discovery and mining of gold in Emerald Gap. The murals had been painted twenty years ago by Rutger Dunlap, a sometime artist and local troublemaker whom one of the Oddfellows had mysteriously turned loose with his paints in the lobby. Rutger had painted the murals and then disappeared from Emerald Gap, later to become a famous artist in Europe—

which made Burly Jones, the Oddfellow who'd allowed
Rutger to paint the murals, feel quite smug. Since then,
anyone who did something incomprehensible that later
turned out to be clever or noteworthy was said in Emerald
Gap to have "pulled a Burly."

Juliet was standing before the murals, thinking of all this
to keep from thinking how close the end of Midsummer
Madness was, when Andrea found her.

"Oh, there you are, Juliet. And with the tickets and
cashboxes, at last." Andrea, with the no-nonsense brisk-
ness born of years of telling small children what to do,
whisked away the tickets and boxes and turned to call to
Reva Reid, who had just slipped through the second set of
oak doors that led into the main part of the hall. "Reva.
Here, Reva. Would you take care of these?"

Reva, dressed in a formal gown that looked as if it owed
more to the thirties than to the gold rush, murmured, "Of
course." She relieved Andrea of the metal boxes and ticket
rolls, then disappeared once again inside the main hall.

Andrea took Juliet by the hand. "Now, wait a moment
here." She stood back from Juliet, her head tipped to the
side. "Let me see. I have it. General Grant?"

Juliet groaned, wondering if Grant could have had
something to do with the gold rush that she herself had forgotten. "Lotta Crabtree. The Drummer Boy," she cor-
rected. "I left my drum in the car for now."

Andrea, who herself seemed to be dressed as a pioneer
woman of some sort, complete with poke bonnet and mus-
lin apron, shook her head. "That simply goes to prove that
even kindergarten teachers don't know everything. Now,
come along. I must show you all that's been accomplished
since you went home to change."

With a rustle of her long gathered skirt, Andrea swooped
toward the second set of double doors and, one at a time,

swung them back and anchored them open with a pair of doorstops. Juliet moved to the open doorway to look. Reva Reid, setting up the parallel ticket tables right beyond the entrance, glanced up and winked. Juliet smiled back and then stood staring, appropriately awed.

Overhead, obscuring the beamed ceiling, gold foil dangled in loops and whorls, glistening in the little spotlights that had been cleverly concealed in every nook, cranny and corner. In the center of all the looped and coiling foil hung a huge nugget made of papier mâché, itself covered with foil so that it sparkled as it slowly turned in the light.

Across the hall from the entrance, the stage where the band would play had been done up to look like a mountain glen, with imitation boulders and plastic bushes and small fresh-cut trees on wooden stands. Down the center of the stage, skirting the piano and the microphone stand, ran a stream made of wrinkled aluminum foil, which gleamed quite convincingly in the light from above. The stream "trickled" off the stage a little left of center, ending rather abruptly when it hit the dance floor.

On one side of the stage stood a mountain of borrowed stereo equipment. Burt Pandley would be putting that to use whenever the band took a break. Burt was highly qualified for the job of choosing recorded dance music, as he'd been a D.J. in Auburn at one time.

The bar, courtesy of McIntyre's, was tucked up on the other side of the stage. Behind it, Archie Kent, wearing a white shirt, red suspenders and a bow tie, was getting ready to open shop.

Juliet sighed and decided it was all quite spectacular and inviting, as well, right down to the little brass lanterns on each of the small conversation tables that surrounded the dance floor.

"What a job you've all done," she told Andrea and Reva, and everyone else within earshot.

Andrea nodded. "We certainly have. It helps to have a proper director, at last."

Juliet smiled a gracious thank-you. Then she pulled back her brass-buttoned cuff and glanced at her watch. It was seven-fifty, and the dance was scheduled to start at eight. People would begin arriving any minute now.

Juliet remembered her drum. "Is everything under control, then?" Reva and Andrea agreed that it was, and Juliet left them to collect the finishing touch of her costume.

Outside, it was still light, though the sun had slipped behind the rim of the mountains a few moments ago. She'd just swung the strap of her drum in place over her chest and locked her car door, when she spied the derelict in long johns coming toward her from the corner of Broad Street.

It took her several seconds to realize who it was: Cody, walking over from his restaurant. As soon as she recognized him, she burst into laughter. They'd both made a game of not telling the other what their costume would be. Leave it to Cody, the best-looking man in Emerald Gap, to get himself up like a vagrant prospector for the Gold Rush Ball.

He wore no pants over the grubby long johns. His boots looked like they'd been salvaged from a trash can. Around his waist, from a wide belt, he'd strung a gold pan and a small pickax. His hat, so battered and torn as to be truly pitiful, had a wide, floppy brim that shaded a face smeared with something gray and sooty, so that it looked as if it had been a long time since he'd shaved. When he got close enough to give her a wide grin, she saw that he'd blacked out a couple of teeth.

"Oh, Cody...."

"Gimme a kiss, woman," he demanded. He grabbed her, right there on the sidewalk, and bent her back over his arm, causing her drum to bang against the parking meter by her car.

"Unhand me, varlet." She giggled and pretended to struggle.

But the derelict prospector would not be refused. In the end, as best she could with a drum strapped across her chest, she gave him the kiss he'd demanded, though he did complain against her mouth that it was hard to believe she was really surrendering when she refused to stop laughing. Around them, as the first partygoers arrived, there were chuckles and shouts of encouragement.

At last, Cody released her and stepped back to study her costume. "Hmm. A soldier from Sutter's Fort?" Sutter's Fort, in Sacramento, was near where the first California gold had been discovered.

Juliet made a disgusted noise in her throat and held her arms out. "You happen to be looking at one of Lotta Crabtree's most beloved impersonations, The Drummer Boy."

Cody continued to look puzzled.

Juliet groaned. "It begins to look as if I won't be winning the Best Costume ribbon this year."

"Well, now, Julie...." He scratched his head through his pitiful hat.

She planted her hands on her hips. "'Well, now, Julie'? Is that all you can say? Do you have any idea how much I spent on this getup?"

He chucked her under the chin. "Settle down. So what if you're unrecognizable? You look terrific. Cutest little soldier I ever saw."

She looked down at herself, then doubtfully up at him. "Right."

"Come on, stop sulking. You're the boss of the party—it's not fair you should expect to win all the prizes, too."

"I just want..." she began, and then didn't finish.

"What?"

Tonight to be perfect, a memory to treasure. For the rest of my life, she thought. But she didn't say it. It sounded much too sad, somehow. And she didn't want to sound sad. She wanted to have a wonderful time.

"What is it, Julie?" His eyes were full of concern.

"It's nothing." Her voice was very bright.

"But, Julie—"

She didn't let him finish. "You're right. I was sulking. And I'm through sulking now." She took his arm and grinned up at him. "Shall we go in, sir?"

For a moment he just looked at her. Then he shrugged and fell in with her banter. "You bet, you little wildcat, you." He led her inside where Reva and Andrea were already busy taking tickets and the band had begun the first set.

Except for the fact that nobody recognized her costume, the first two hours of the dance were pure pleasure for Juliet. She beat on her drum and kicked up her heels, joining right in with the line dances even though she didn't know the steps.

Whenever a slow number started up, Andrea let her slip the drum beneath one of the ticket tables. Then Cody would lead her out on the floor and pull her into his arms and it was simply heaven. Not only was she close against his body, which she loved, but Cody was such a great dancer that he made even Juliet, who'd never had the opportunity to learn much about dancing, look like she knew what she was doing.

It wasn't until a little after ten, when the dance floor swarmed with costumed dancers and most of the tables on the sidelines were full, that things began to get rough.

First, there was a big commotion out in the lobby. When Juliet followed the problem to its source, she learned that someone—no one had seen who—had painted a purple moustache on a gold panner on one of the Rutger Dunlap murals. Burly Jones, now well into his seventies and costumed for the ball as the front half of a mule—Evan McMulch II being the other half—stood in the middle of the lobby ranting and raving and declaring, "A priceless treasure has been defaced!"

With considerable effort, Juliet finally pushed her way through the growing group of gawkers to reach Burly's side.

"Mr. Jones—"

"Don't bother me, girl. A tragedy has occurred here! What has befallen our fair town, for such a thing to be allowed to happen, under the very noses of those of us that care the most! I ask you all, to what pass have we come?"

Juliet, who had smelled 80 proof when Burly turned to her, tried tugging on his arm, under which was tucked the mule head he had recently removed. "Mr. Jones, if we could discuss this in private—"

"Private! Private, you say? I won't be silenced, never. I'll shout it to the rooftops. A sacred treasure has been defiled!"

"But, Mr. Jones, we *are* insured. All damages will be covered, I promise."

Burly turned his rather bulging eyes on Juliet and released another fumy breath. "Money? You talk of mere money? This is *art* that has been destroyed here—our history, our past...."

Juliet almost gave in and left Burly Jones to rant and rave to his heart's content. But then she glanced to the side and saw Cody, an ironic grin on his face, giving her the lifted eyebrow that she knew meant, *Do you need some help?* She shook her head, reinforced by the simple knowledge that he was there.

This time, she took Burly firmly by the arm and began to walk. Though he continued to rant, he did go where she pulled him, which was through a side door into the small office at the front of the building. There, with no audience, he was at least willing to grudgingly listen as she promised that, though of course money couldn't replace the priceless mural, money *could* make certain that it was properly restored.

After Burly's feathers were effectively smoothed, Juliet returned to the lobby where all was now quiet. She then posted a volunteer guard on a folding chair to see that the murals received no further embellishments.

At last, near eleven, she reentered the hall to find Burt Pandley announcing the commencement of the competition for Best Costume, male and female. Andrea Oakleaf and Reva Reid, he explained, the two trusty ticket takers, had already acted as preliminary judges, since they'd seen everyone at least once when they came in the door.

At that point, Andrea and Reva were asked to step up onto the stage and, their feet in the aluminum creek, the two ladies took turns reading off their choices. Though she held out little hope of winning, Juliet grabbed her drum and drumsticks from beneath the ticket table anyway, so that she would be fully attired just in case a miracle happened and her name was called.

The miracle failed to occur. But Juliet found she didn't mind too much, especially when Cody was one of the finalists. She clapped and hooted with the best of them when he climbed up on the stage. He looked so totally absurd in his long johns and battered hat.

When all the nominees were named, there were four men and four women contestants crammed up on the stage, as well as the master of ceremonies, Burt. Reva and Andrea had thoughtfully stepped down. Burt then held the microphone over each contender's head, gauging the success of the costume by the strength of the applause.

Cody lost out to Yardley Forbes, who'd got himself up as the doomed Maria Elena, in a dress that was a man-size duplicate of the one Yolanda Hughes wore in the revue, with a noose around his neck and a lot of blue face paint—so that he would look as if he'd already been hanged.

The woman who won—a redhead in a gorgeous dance hall-girl costume—looked familiar to Juliet. It wasn't until the woman grabbed Cody, who happened to be standing beside her when her victory was announced, and kissed him, that Juliet remembered her as the fiery-haired woman from McIntyre's the Wednesday before.

Cody pretended to reel from the woman's kiss, and then to recover himself enough to grin his black-toothed grin at the wave of hoots and catcalls that followed. Juliet, watching, knew he was only playing to the audience, not encouraging the beautiful redhead in the least. Still, seeing him kissing someone else touched her where she was most vulnerable.

The sadness she was trying to keep down rose up once more. It was Saturday night. Not much time left. Her fantasy was coming to an end. Midsummer Madness was almost over. Tomorrow night, she and Cody would talk about where they were going from here.

Up on the stage, Burt was pinning the blue ribbon to the beautiful redhead's silky bodice. The redhead was smiling seductively at Cody. The crowd hooted and stomped.

Juliet, who felt unwelcome tears rise to her eyes, began grimly reminding herself of the reality of the situation.

Cody was a wonderful person. He was kind, and he'd always looked out for her. But that didn't make him hers, not the way she wanted him to be.

He might handle Billy Butley for her. He might encourage her to dive off the high rock down at the South Fork swimming hole. He might do her the ultimate kindness and teach her the mysteries of passion and desire. He might even want her, for a brief time, before someone more beautiful, more self-assured, came along and stole him away.

But the reality was that Juliet Huddleston would never be able to hold a man like Cody McIntyre. She simply must make herself come to grips with that fact.

Beyond the press of people in front of her, the stage grew more blurry with each passing moment. Juliet dashed away the foolish tears. Then, adjusting the leather strap so that her drum hung behind her, she turned to make her way through the press of people to the lobby and the rest room. Once safely there, she could lock herself into a stall for a few minutes until her shaky emotions were back under control.

But she didn't make it, because halfway there, Andrea Oakleaf met up with her.

"There you are. We've got a little problem."

"Oh, Andrea...." She longed to just beg off, but then she remembered that, as the director of the festival, problems that others couldn't solve fell to her. She shifted the big drum to the side again, where it was more comfortable when she was standing still. "What is it?"

Andrea leaned toward her and spoke in a low voice. "When Reva and I were up on stage, Melda was watching the door for us...."

"Yes?"

"And somehow..."

"What? Tell me."

Andrea finally got it out. "Someone appears to have stolen one of the cashboxes."

"Oh, Lord."

"I know. It's terrible."

"How much was in it?"

"About half of tonight's take—and the fifty in change that we started with."

"Did anybody see anything?"

"Not that we can find out. Melda was just using the one box, while we were on the stage. She asked Evan McMulch to watch the other one, but he had had a lot to drink, and appears to have wandered off, leaving the box unguarded. Evidently, for several minutes, no one was paying any attention to the box."

Juliet considered. All told, the festival had been the biggest money-maker ever. And the ball was supposed to be the crowning glory of the ten days of fun. "Look. We can afford to lose the money better than we can afford to ruin the ball, don't you think?"

"Yes," Andrea said. "Yes, I agree."

"So let's get a few people together to look, but keep it low-key, fair enough?"

Andrea nodded. "Very wise, I would say."

However that was not to be, because poor Melda, in a dither over what had happened under her very nose, had mentioned the problem to more than one person before she reported it to Andrea and Reva. And, just as Juliet and Andrea agreed to keep things quiet, Burly Jones began decrying the theft from over near the entrance doors.

Juliet, grimly pushing her drum behind her again, turned to jostle her way through the crowd and deal with Burly one more time. She was just pulling on the arm that held the mule's head again, to lead Burly to the front office where she could calm him down, when there was a cry from out near the double doors to the street.

She glanced that way, through the hall doors and across the lobby, and there was Flat-nosed Jake, locked in a tussle with Evan McMulch II. Evan, still dressed as the back half of the mule to which Burly was the front, clutched the missing cashbox and whined piteously that he hadn't done anything wrong.

"My God," Burly breathed beside her. "It's Evan. Evan is the culprit. To what a pass has this world come?"

Juliet very calmly took off her drum and held it out to Burly. "Hold this, would you?"

For once Burly Jones was shocked enough to simply do as he was told. He took the big drum in his free hand and Juliet hurried across the lobby to help Flat-nosed Jake.

Fifteen minutes later, as midnight approached, Juliet finally felt she had the story straight. Melda had asked Evan to watch the spare cashbox for her, and Evan, feeling the call of nature, had taken the box with him to the men's room in the front of the building off the lobby. Once in the rest room, Evan had found that he was feeling a little ill—perhaps he'd had just one too many bourbons on the rocks, he was willing to admit—and so he'd sat down on the waste bin to wait for the room to stop whirling around. When he collected himself enough to venture out again, he'd been ruthlessly attacked by Flat-nosed Jake and accused of all manner of heinous crimes.

After the whole story was out, Juliet spent a while soothing Evan's hurt pride and reassuring Jake that he'd done the right thing. At last, everyone seemed to come down to earth and accept the fact that it had all been nothing more than a massive misunderstanding.

Praying that nothing else would go wrong with her "perfect" evening, Juliet returned to the ballroom just as the fiddle player was announcing the last waltz of the evening. "Grab your special lady, gents. Because this is it for the Gold Rush Ball for another year...."

Juliet, wanting the last waltz with Cody more than just about anything right then, scanned the crowded room for his disreputable hat. He saw her just as she saw him, and he started elbowing his way toward her through the throng. The smile of anticipation on his grimy face lifted her spirits and soothed her frazzled nerves. The ball might not have been exactly as she might have dreamed, but at least she would have the last waltz with Cody to remember when everything was done.

Cody was less than fifteen feet from her when the beautiful redhead in the dance hall-girl costume materialized out of nowhere and laid her slim hand on his arm. "How about the last dance, handsome?"

Cody smiled politely at her. "No, ma'am. I have a partner." He shook her hand off.

But too many strangers nearby had seen the redhead kiss Cody up there on the stage. The hoots and hollers began.

"Give the lady the last dance, you fool!"

"Don't turn down an offer like that!"

"What are you, man? Certifiable?"

Cody gently said no again and shrugged off the gibes. He kept coming toward Juliet. Jokingly, one man grabbed him, and then another joined in. "Dance with the lady," they demanded, caught up in the moment, and perhaps pushing the joke a little too far.

Cody was beginning to look angry. "Look, folks. Back off, okay?"

Juliet, who'd had enough hassles for one evening, decided it would be wiser to give in. She sent Cody a regretful look, then mouthed the words, "Dance with her. It's okay."

He narrowed his eyes at her and said again, "No."

"Please. Just do it."

He stared at her for a moment, an unreadable expression on his face, while the hecklers who held him badgered him some more. Then, finally, he shrugged. "Okay. Fine."

He was immediately released and pushed in the direction of the beautiful redhead. She gave him a come-hither smile. He held out his hand and led her out on the floor.

Juliet stood on the sidelines and watched them for a moment. Even with Cody wearing his silly costume, they were still the two most beautiful people in the room. They might have been made for each other.

"Share the last waltz with old Jake?" Flat-nosed Jake was grinning at her. Juliet smiled back at him and followed him out on the floor.

Soon enough, the dance ended. Jake gave her a courtly bow.

"That's all, folks. See you next year," the fiddle player announced. There was a round of applause, and then Burt took the microphone once again to remind everyone of the closing day picnic tomorrow and the final performance of the Midsummer Madness Revue tomorrow night.

Burt Pandley left the stage. The regular hall lights came up.

Juliet blinked at the sudden brightness, and when she opened her eyes, all the painted faces around her looked garish and haggard. Up on the stage, a couple of the trees had toppled, their pine stands naked and raw looking in the harsh light. The tinfoil stream, torn and trampled by too many high-heeled shoes, made a pathetic sight. Above, a lot of the looped foil had come loose and hung in sad tendrils all around the hall.

The Gold Rush Ball was over. Slowly the movement of the crowd toward the exits began.

Jake gave Juliet a quick peck on the cheek and murmured something about getting things straightened up enough to leave, then he was gone.

Juliet, feeling disoriented, tried to remember what she had to do next. Not much, really. Babe Allen would take care of the cashboxes, since she was treasurer of the festival this year. And Jake was responsible for locking up, while a volunteer cleanup crew would put the place to rights at nine the next morning.

Her drum. That was it. She had to get her drum from Burly Jones. Juliet turned to look for Burly—and came up short against Cody's hard chest.

"Hey, imagine running into you here." Cody laughed, a warm, masculine sound that, for some stupid reason, made Juliet want to cry all over again. She looked down, in a frantic effort to get her emotions back in control. "Julie?" Cody took her by the arms. "Julie, what the hell is bothering you?"

"Nothing. Nothing, really." She flashed him a blinding smile and wriggled free of his grip. "I have to get my drum. Burly's got it somewhere."

"Julie, wait...."

She was already moving away from him, calling over her shoulder. "I'll meet you at my car. Fifteen minutes, okay?"

She didn't hear his answer and right then it didn't matter. All she wanted was a little time, to get her feelings back in line. Then everything would be fine. She was sure of it. They'd have their final beautiful night together. Her last memory to treasure, for the rest of her days.

Ten

"Look, Julie. I can't take this anymore. What the hell is going on?"

They'd just arrived at the ranch house after the dance and were standing in the big foyer at the foot of the stairs. It was past 2:00 a.m.

Cody had ridden home with her in her car. It had been a long, silent ride—except for the knocking sound from the engine, of course. Juliet, who had meant to put her sad feelings behind her, had not succeeded in the least.

All during the ride, she kept picturing Cody and the redhead, whirling across the dance floor in the last waltz. And the more she pictured them dancing, the more she had to admit that she was jealous of the redhead, though Cody had done absolutely nothing to encourage the woman. In fact, if anyone had encouraged the woman, it had been Juliet herself. Cody had been clearly unwilling; he'd wanted to dance with Juliet. But Juliet had turned him down. Under the pretext of avoiding trouble, she'd pushed him right into the other woman's arms.

Oh, she didn't understand her own actions lately. It was as if she were...falling apart. As if the new, assertive woman she'd thought she'd become was just a false shell, now cracking, to expose a forlorn real self who huddled, fearful and confused, inside.

"Julie, talk to me."

Juliet, utterly miserable, looked down at her black soldier's boots and said nothing.

"Damn it, look at me."

She forced herself to look in his eyes. "I...I can't talk about it right now, Cody. I don't understand it myself. Please...." Her voice trailed off. Please what? She didn't know.

The limit of Cody's patience was unquestionably within view. "Great. Terrific," he said, and skimmed off his ragged hat to send it sailing through the doorway to his right, into the living room, where it landed on a recliner. "At first, you won't talk to me until Sunday. And now, you say you *can't* talk to me. I don't get it. I don't get it at all."

He shook his head, making a low sound of frustration in his throat, and then he followed his hat into the living room, where he dropped to the big sectional sofa. Juliet, despising herself by then, just stayed in the foyer staring after him woefully. After a minute, he craned his head to look back at her. "Well? Are you going to stand in the hall all night or what?"

Juliet obediently trudged into the living room.

He gave her a pushed-to-the-limit look. "Sit down."

She dropped to a straight chair. Cody looked at her some more, waiting for her to say something. When she didn't, he asked, "Why have you been moping around all night, looking like you want to cry one minute, and then pasting on a big smile and swearing it's nothing when I ask you what's wrong?"

"Oh, Cody..."

"What?"

"I don't know."

"That's not good enough. Tell me what's wrong."

She didn't answer. It seemed pointless. She'd only be repeating what she'd said before.

"Then answer another question." He tried again. "Why in hell did you shove that redheaded woman at me for the last dance? Are you trying to tell me something here, is that it?"

She managed to mutter, "I just thought it would be better, to avoid trouble." It was a coward's lie. Her shame increased.

"Better in what way?" he demanded. "Better if I dance the last dance with some woman I don't even know?"

"No, no, of course not."

"Then what?"

"Oh, Cody...."

"Answer me."

"Cody, it was only a dance."

"'Only a dance.'" He repeated the words with a sneer. "You wanted that dance. At least, the way you looked at me said you wanted that dance. Did I read you wrong?"

"Okay. Yes, I wanted the dance. But there were just...all these hassles tonight. The mustache on the mural, and Evan McMulch and the cashbox. I didn't want another hassle."

"I wanted to dance with you, and you wanted to dance with me. All you had to do was step forward, and those idiots who were after me would have left it alone. But instead, you stepped back. Why, Julie? Why did you do that?" He stood up then and came to loom over her. "Answer me. Why?"

"I just..." She gazed up at him, desolate. He should have looked absurd, in his long johns with his blacked-out teeth. But he didn't. He looked so achingly handsome that it hurt just to look at him. So handsome. So far out of her league. "Please. Please, not now."

"When then?"

"Tomorrow night...."

"Oh," he said with heavy sarcasm. "That's right, tomorrow night. Tomorrow night's the big night when you'll finally talk to me."

"We agreed—"

He loosed an expletive. "*We* didn't do anything. *You* told me how it would be, and then anytime I wanted to make things different, you'd change the subject or suddenly have to be somewhere else."

Juliet looked at him, admitting to herself that he was right, and feeling ashamed. She knew exactly what she should do: start right now with honesty. She should tell him everything, from the love in her heart for him, to her absolute conviction that someday she would lose him to someone more desirable.

The room was very quiet. Outside, Kemo, who had been left on the porch, whined to get in.

"Cody...." Juliet began, determined at last to tell all. A single tear trickled from her lid and trailed down her cheek.

"Damn it, Julie," Cody muttered. He reached out and wiped the tear away, the touch infinitely gentle.

"Oh, Cody, I..." She sought the right words, the honest words, that would get it all out in the open for good and all.

But then she saw the tenderness in his face. The sight of her tears had softened him, made him more vulnerable. He'd lost track of his goal to get her to talk.

It was truly her moment of choice. She could go ahead and tell him the secrets of her heart. Or she could claim what was left of her final night of fantasy.

She lifted her arms, rising toward him. "Please, Cody. Hold me."

With a low growl, he enfolded her, pulling her against his hard body, and lowering his mouth to hers. Juliet kissed him eagerly, hungrily, all her unspoken love and longing expressed in the heat and hunger of her lips beneath his.

As the kiss spun out into eternity, Cody swung her up against his chest and headed for the stairs and his own wide bed.

In his room, he set her down long enough to slip the brass buttons of her uniform through their holes, and slide her jacket off, to strip her of her boots, push down her soldier's pants, to peel away every wisp of cloth that protected her from his sight. He was out of his own absurd costume in no time at all.

Then he lay her down upon the bed and made love to her with a fierceness and heat that burned her down to pure sensation and made her beg him hoarsely to never, ever stop.

When the time came that he rose up over her and poised to bury himself in her softness, she cried out and reached for him. He came down upon her. She welcomed him eagerly. Slowly at first, then with building momentum, their bodies began the ultimate dance of love.

When her fulfillment came, she gloried in it, thrashing wildly beneath him, so that he, too, lost himself in the final, spinning vortex of shared pleasure.

Afterward, they lay, sweating bodies entwined. And Juliet rubbed her moist cheek against his shoulder, kissed him and tried not to think that she had made the coward's choice.

But she had. She'd chosen her fantasy, her final night of passion, over the harsh purity of truth.

Morning came too soon. Juliet woke alone in Cody's bed. Groggy and bewildered, she called to him. But no answer came. She pulled on his robe that hung behind the door and went to look for him, but the rooms were all empty.

Apprehension filled her. Had something happened; was something wrong?

She returned to Cody's bedroom and dressed in her wrinkled soldier's costume. Then she went out to the front porch, where Kemo waited to be scratched behind the ear. She petted the dog.

Bud Southey, the caretaker, who lived in a small set of rooms behind the garage, was over by the pool. Wondering if he might know something, she called to him.

Bud crossed the driveway and stood at the foot of the steps. "Yes, ma'am," he said, when she asked if he knew where Cody had gone. "Left about an hour ago. Said to tell you he decided to go on into town by himself this morning. Drove his old pickup."

It took Juliet a moment to absorb that information. "But why?" she asked at last.

Bud shrugged. "Well, ma'am, I didn't see as how it was my place to ask." The words were courteous, but pointed.

"Oh," she said, feeling her face color a little. Bud had always been a quiet, self-contained sort of fellow. He wasn't the type to get involved in his boss's private affairs. "Yes, of course. I see. Thank you, Bud."

"Welcome, ma'am." Bud politely tipped his baseball cap at her and went back to the pool, where he picked up the long-poled strainer and began sweeping the surface of the clear water.

For a moment more, Juliet absently stroked Kemo's sleek coat and tried to push down her growing anxiety. Perhaps something had come up concerning the restaurant or the hardware store—perhaps a break-in or something like that.

But that didn't add up. She would have heard the phone by the bed if it had rung; she was sure of it.

At last, accepting the fact that she could learn nothing by standing on the porch worrying and wondering, she felt in her pocket for her car keys. Then she told Kemo to stay, went down the steps to her car and drove it back to her house.

There, she showered and dressed. She put on her makeup. She ate breakfast—an egg, toast, juice, and coffee. A busy day lay before her, and she needed the food, especially considering how little sleep she'd had.

Sipping her second cup of coffee, Juliet glanced at her watch. Nine o'clock. In half an hour, she was due at Pine Grove Park. Though Andrea was in charge of the picnic and had enlisted a crew of seven to meet her at the crack of dawn to get things set up, Juliet was expected to oversee the final steps of the process. She should get going very soon.

But what about Cody? She needed to talk to him, find out what was going on, why he'd gotten up from bed and vanished without a word, leaving her nothing but the caretaker's brief message.

She picked up the phone and dialed the hardware store. After two rings, a machine answered and Elma Lou Bealer's voice listed the store hours and urged her to leave a message after the beep.

"Cody," Juliet said into the phone. "Cody, are you there? It's me, Juliet...." She began to feel like a fool; Elma Lou would probably pick up the messages tomorrow morning, and hear the frustration and confusion in her voice.

Juliet cleared her throat and said swiftly. "Please call me." Then she hung up.

Next, she tried the restaurant, but this time she planned what she would say in her message before she dialed. Once again, she got a recording, so she waited for the beep.

"Cody, it's Juliet. I must speak with you. I think I can find some time after I check in with Andrea at the park. So if you happen to get this, would you please just...stay there and wait for me?"

Cody, sitting at his desk in the office of his deserted restaurant and staring at the answering machine as it recorded Juliet's voice on the other end of the line, grunted.

"Um, thank you." From the machine, there was a click, a dial tone and then the sounds of the tape rewinding as the thing reset itself.

Cody shifted his focus from the source of Juliet's voice to his booted feet, which were crossed on his desk not far from the machine. Next to his boots steamed an untouched cup of coffee.

Cody was a man who rarely got mad. But he was mad now. Madder than hell. At Juliet Huddleston.

He'd awakened next to her at a little after seven. Sleeping, she had looked as innocent as a child. He'd smoothed a few strands of hair away from her face and kissed her once lightly. She'd smiled and stirred but hadn't opened her eyes.

Lying there against her, he'd thought about their lovemaking the night before and felt himself getting aroused all over again.

And then he'd remembered how the lovemaking had started. How he'd begged her to talk to him, and she'd put him off the way she always did. How she'd finally cried a little, to soften him up. And then put her arms around him, offering him her sweet kiss—and once again he'd learned nothing of what was bothering her.

That was why he'd left without a word this morning. He'd needed to be alone. So he could decide what the hell was going on here, not to mention what he was going to do about it.

Cody recrossed his boots and looked at them some more.

Okay, maybe he was being a callous jerk. Maybe he should have been more understanding of whatever was going on with her that she didn't trust him enough to explain. Maybe last night he shouldn't have pressured her so hard.

Cody swung his boots to the floor and picked up his coffee. He brought the cup to his lips—and then set it down without drinking and stared off toward the door with unseeing eyes.

And maybe this morning he should have kissed her awake and held her tenderly and begged her one more time to tell him what the hell was going on in her head.

But he was getting damned tired of begging. And he wasn't going to feel guilty for the things he hadn't done, for not being more understanding last night, and not hanging around to try again this morning. Why the hell should he keep trying to get through to her, when he knew damn well what was bothering her and just didn't want to admit it to himself?

Cody grabbed the coffee again and blew on it to cool it.

Yeah, he knew what it was all right. He might as well face it. She was calling it off between them . . . tonight.

He was sure that was it. Why else would she have thrown some other woman at him, unless she was hoping the other woman might take him off her hands? It made depressing sense, if he just faced up to it. She'd been mooning around like a motherless calf all through the dance last night because she knew what she planned to do, and she dreaded hurting him.

That was how Julie was. She never wanted to hurt a soul—not even a man she was trying to get rid of.

Cody drank from his cup. The coffee scalded his lip, and he swore when he set the brew down.

He was mad as hell at her. She'd had her fantasy, just the way she'd wanted it, and now she was ready to get back to real life.

She was planning to dump him; he knew it. And she thought doing a lot of suffering over it would somehow make it okay. She probably expected, when she finally dropped the news on him, that he'd feel so sorry for her because she was so upset, he'd forget all about the fact that he was the one getting dumped.

Good old Cody McIntyre, he thought with considerable ire. A gentleman to the end. And, of course, he'd always been a gentleman before, with women. Julie, who'd known him all his life, would expect him to be the same with her.

But that was the point, he'd realized just now. It wasn't the same with her. Nothing, at all, was the same with her.

Cody swung his boots back up on his desk and stared at them some more. She had a surprise coming, he decided. Because he wasn't going take this lying down.

And he wasn't going to be here waiting when she came looking for him, either. Let her have a little taste of her own medicine today. Let her try to talk to him and find just how busy *he* could be....

There was trouble at Pine Grove Park. The moment Juliet arrived, Andrea came rushing over to the car, her expression harried and her gray bun askew.

"Juliet. At last. I was beginning to think you'd never get here."

Juliet, who'd barely managed to climb from the car before Andrea descended on her, shut her door behind her and grimly accepted the fact that her plans for seeking out Cody might have to be changed. "What's wrong?"

"Everything. Only four of the seven on my setup crew showed up on time. Edna Coombes hasn't come yet. And she's supposed to bring the folding tables from the town hall. And you know Melda's second cousin from Roseville?"

"Our professional auctioneer for the pie auction?"

"The very one. He's begged off."

"Oh, no."

"Oh, yes. Melda just came over to tell me. Poor thing. She feels terrible. First, Evan staggered off with the cashbox when she was supposed to be in charge of it last night, and now her cousin backs out on her. She was almost in tears, and swore that that cousin of hers was never a person one could depend on— Heaven knows why she waited until now to say that, but I didn't have the heart to point that out. She looked mortified enough as it was."

"I understand," Juliet soothed. "Anything else?"

"We're still waiting for the complimentary meats and buns from Steerman's Grocery."

"And?"

"The paper products. The charcoal briquettes."

"Has *anything* arrived on time?"

Andrea sighed. "The tablecloths are here—too bad we don't have the tables to put them on."

"Okay," Juliet said. "How many vehicles do we have?"

Andrea quickly counted and told her, and Juliet began assigning errands to everyone with a car.

Juliet herself drove over to Steerman's Grocery to see what had happened to the meat and the buns. The assistant manager, on duty at the time, claimed he knew nothing about a contribution to the picnic. The manager was called, and the assistant manager had a very red face by the time he hung up the phone.

Steerman's delivery truck was immediately requisitioned and filled with every manner of hot dog and burger and bun imaginable. The truck followed Juliet directly to Pine Grove Park.

By then, the tables had arrived, and Andrea's crew was busy setting them up. Juliet was helping wherever she was needed when it suddenly occurred to her that Burt Pandley, with his experience as a disc jockey, might pinch-hit just fine as a pie auctioneer.

She got in her car again and drove to a pay phone. Burt was a late sleeper and she ended up getting him out of bed. But he came awake rather quickly when she asked for his help.

"You betcha. Be glad to. I can be there in an hour."

Juliet looked at her watch. It was eleven-thirty and the auction was slated for one. It would be close but better than nothing. She thanked Burt profusely before she said good-bye.

After she hung up, Juliet just stood there, her hand still on the phone. It was her first quiet moment since Andrea had come flying out to meet her at her car.

She thought of Cody and wondered again what had happened to make him leave her this morning without a word. But the picnic was officially starting in just half an hour. It was her job to be there, at least until things were effectively underway.

Since she had the phone, she called the restaurant, the hardware store and the ranch, too. Cody didn't answer any of the calls.

Well, she decided grimly, she'd done what she could for now. She had to get back for the beginning of the picnic.

Then, maybe, she could steal a little time away. She'd track Cody down, and they'd talk.

But Cody surprised her. He was there, at the park, tied into a white apron and grilling the first round of burgers and hot dogs when Juliet returned.

Hesitantly, she approached him. "Cody?"

He turned those gray-green eyes on her and something in her midsection turned over and then melted. "Yeah?"

"I..."

"What?"

"Where did you go?"

"When?"

"This morning."

"I told Bud to tell you."

"Into town?"

"That's right." He turned back to the grill.

She stared at his profile for a moment, wondering what to do next. He was being so...uncommunicative about this, so unlike his usual kind, attentive self.

"But, Cody...." She tried again.

"Yeah?"

She glanced around at the other three grills where volunteers were flipping burgers, at the tables laden with food, and all the people nearby bustling to get things in order. She knew this was neither the time nor the place.

"Um," she began, "after things get going here...in an hour or so? Could you and I talk?"

He flipped a burger over, and then set a few buns to warm on the edge of the grill. Then, after what seemed like forever, he said, "What do you think? These look done to you?" He pointed with the grill spatula.

"Fine. Did you hear what I asked?"

He gave her another look, a brief, distant one, and then he turned back to the grill again. "What was that now?"

"I want to talk. Maybe after the pie auction, or whenever..." Her voice faded off the way it used to.

He looked at her again, then back at his burgers. "You want to talk?"

"Yes." She spoke more firmly. "Yes, I do."

"Sure, Julie. We'll talk."

"When?"

"As soon as I can find the time." He gestured at the grill. "Right now I'm busy."

"Well, I know, but—"

She didn't get to finish, because Babe Allen appeared and grabbed her arm. "Juliet. Andrea tells me it's been a *circus*. But you took care of it. We are so fortunate to have discovered you. Now, come here with me and take a look at these salads...."

Juliet was dragged without further hesitation to the long folding tables, where the potluck dishes of half the women in town were slowly being set out. She exclaimed, rather limply, over everything from Madge Wireman's Three Bean Delight to Lelah McMulch's Tropical Surprise.

After that, she was informed that the reporter from the *Sacramento Bee* had returned, to do a follow-up article on the final day of the festival. She spoke to him, answering all of his questions with a determined smile and then turning him over to Jake, who would stick by him and see that he was entertained for the rest of the day.

By then it was one o'clock, and Burt Pandley was up on the grandstand stage, auctioning off pies and telling corny jokes and doing a great job of it. Several people remarked that Burt was "at least as good as that no-show professional." Melda, who happened to be within earshot, burst into tears and ran for the alder grove by the pond.

Andrea, standing by Juliet, whispered in her ear. "It would mean more if you talked to her than anyone."

So Juliet went after Melda, who cried on her shoulder and declared that she'd nearly ruined the festival twice. Juliet calmed her, swearing it wasn't so, reminding her of the rousing success of her play about Maria Elena and pointing out that everything had worked out fine in the end.

At last, Melda allowed herself to be soothed. Juliet led her back to where the crowd was, and Andrea immediately took over, handing Melda a paper plate and ordering her to get in line for lunch.

After that, things seemed to be under control. Juliet looked around for Cody, but he had disappeared. Later, she saw him throwing horseshoes with Evan McMulch and Burly Jones. She approached and asked him quietly if they might talk now.

Burly, who'd just thrown a ringer, shot her a warning glare. "Don't go bothering him, girl. This here game will be played right through."

Cody gave her a remote smile. "Sorry, Julie. Haven't got the time just yet."

It was that way for the rest of the day. Either Cody was in the middle of something, or he was nowhere to be found. Juliet grew more frustrated as the hours passed, but it did no good. He remained unavailable. At the corner of her consciousness, she began to admit that the way he avoided her could mean only one thing; it was ending between them, as she'd always known it would.

That evening, at home, as she got dressed for the final night of the revue, she longed to just put on her pajamas, climb in her lonely bed, pull the covers over her head and indulge in a week-long crying jag.

But that was impossible. She had responsibilities to fulfill.

Somewhat defiantly, she donned her reddest dress—a snug-fitting knit with a strapless top and a bolero jacket to match. She wore the red high heels that Cody had sneered about that night he'd driven her home when her car wouldn't start, before they'd become lovers—a lifetime ago.

At the auditorium, before the curtain went up, she gave a final pep talk to the cast. Cody stood in the back, watching, looking distant and withdrawn. Juliet tried not to look at him, because just the sight of him made her ache inside.

The revue went off beautifully. Yolanda was in especially good form. There wasn't a dry eye in the house when she uttered her final goodbyes as Maria Elena and then gave herself up to be hung.

As they always did, the members of the audience went wild with enthusiasm during Cody's first song. Juliet managed to stand in her place at the back and listen to that one. But when he strummed the first notes of the haunting ballad he sang in the second act, she felt the dangerous tightness in her throat and quickly slipped out into the lobby before she disgraced herself and burst into tears.

She reentered the auditorium just as the Gap High Madrigals were finishing their closing number. After that, there was a standing ovation and a never-ending curtain call. But at last, the curtain came down on the final performance of the Midsummer Madness Revue. Then Babe Allen got up and thanked everyone who'd had anything even remotely to do with the festival.

Finally Babe announced, "And there's one person, in particular, without whom this year's tremendous success would not have been possible. Let's get her up here to say a few words.... Juliet, come on up!"

Juliet, standing in the back, watched as people craned around to look for the indispensable person that Babe Allen was talking about: herself. It was a moment she'd always dreamed of—a major acknowledgment for a job well done. She should be ecstatic.

But instead, she felt exhausted and bleak. She needed sleep badly. Midsummer Madness was ending; it was over between her and Cody. She didn't want to get up and be gracious before all these people. She just wanted to go home.

Reva Reid, who stood next to her by the door, nudged her and murmured, "Juliet, go on...."

"Juliet," Babe urged with a wave of her arm. "Get on up here!"

Reva gave her a gentle shove. Juliet, moving automatically, started down the aisle for the stage. All around her were staring faces. Tottering a little on her high heels, she mounted the stage from the side, stepped up to the microphone and opened her mouth.

"Th-thank you," she managed to murmur. A few people clapped, a signal of support.

A brief speech took shape in her mind, and she gave it. "It's been challenging, exciting, rewarding and most of all, fun. I honestly wish it would never end. But everything does, I know. I'll just look forward to next year—when we can do it all again!"

And that was enough. The audience burst once more into a rousing round of applause.

Relief flooded through her, surprising her with its force. Deep in her heart, she had feared that she wouldn't be able to speak, that a scene from her worst nightmare would unfold before her. That somehow she would discover that she'd lost the ability she'd worked so hard to gain, the ability to get up in front of a crowd and make herself heard.

But that had not happened. And that was good to know.

Bowing once graciously, she turned and walked off into the wings just as someone raised the curtain again and all the performers came back onstage for a final closing-night bow. Juliet stood on the sidelines, clapping heartily for the others one more time.

At last it was truly over. Except for her final thank-you to the cast and crew, which she gave in the dressing room before everyone went home. Cody, as before, stood in the back while she spoke, his beautiful face cold and expressionless. Glancing his way once was enough. She got the message; the long-awaited talk between them would not be taking place that night. It was over, and that was that.

Juliet looked away from Cody and finished her final speech of the night. "Thank you all, for everything. And please try out again next year."

"Hold it there, Juliet." Flat-nosed Jake spoke up from near the doorway.

Juliet felt a slight lifting of her spirits at the sound of her friend's voice. She smiled. "What is it, Jake?"

"I want everyone to come on out to my place. I'm throwing a closing-night party. And you all better be there."

A fresh wave of excitement passed through the group. Most of them were too keyed up to go home and sleep, anyway. Jake began distributing maps to his big cabin out in the woods.

Juliet herself longed only to go home. But in the milling confusion as everyone got ready to leave, more than one person urged her to go to the party. And when Jake caught her arm and demanded her presence, she found she couldn't bring herself to refuse, though she was tired to the bone.

Jake, who usually saw to locking up, asked Juliet if she would take care of it tonight so he could go early and get ready for the party. Juliet agreed and thus found herself leaving the auditorium after everyone else had already gone.

She anticipated a long, lonely ride out there. But that wasn't exactly how it turned out. Because just as she pulled out of the auditorium's deserted parking lot, Cody's pickup fell in behind her.

Juliet's tiredness and frustration redoubled. He wouldn't talk to her, he walked away whenever she came near, but now he was going to shadow her all the way out to Jake's. What was the matter with him? Had he no heart at all?

It would serve him right if she slammed on the brakes, jumped out of her car and marched back there to demand to know what he was up to. But she wouldn't. He'd only say she didn't own the highway, and then where would she be?

No, better to ignore him.

Juliet defiantly slipped a tape into the deck and cranked up the car stereo. She sang along so loudly that her throat was burning by the time she turned off the main road and onto the twisting, two-lane highway that eventually would take her to Jake's place.

She drove deeper into the woods, where the tall trees grew close to the highway, so dense in some places that the night sky could not be seen. Cody's headlights, behind her, were the only proof she was not totally alone. The thought that he was the only one besides herself for miles brought on a fresh onslaught of misery. He was right behind her—yet they might as well be on different planets, with the distance that lay between them now.

She cranked up the stereo another notch and continued to shout along.

Whenever she came to a fork in the road, she'd shift down to be ready in case it was a place the map said to turn. And every time she did that, Cody's black pickup would loom up very close behind her. Once, he even honked at her, impatiently, to let her know she was driving erratically. But what else could she do? The small, wooden signposts were hard to read through the blur of her tears.

She was about two-thirds of the way there and looking for the next turnoff, when she saw one coming up and shifted down. But it wasn't the turn shown on the map after all. She shifted back up to a higher gear, pressing the accelerator, getting up to speed once again.

Right at that moment, something awful happened to her car, something she could hear even over the blaring of her stereo. The noise under the hood went mad, as if someone had taken a crowbar and decided to beat the engine to death with it. There was a lot of crunching. Then a huge, cataclysmic clunk.

Her car stopped dead in the middle of the road. Cody, behind her, skidded to keep from hitting her, pulled to the left, and ended up on the shoulder.

In the silence after both vehicles had stopped, Juliet's car stereo continued to bray, playing that song about a woman with legs who knew how to use them. After a few moments of that, Juliet reached out and silenced it.

And then, suffused suddenly with the kind of dead calm that occurs at the eye of a storm, she leaned on her steering wheel and stared through the windshield at the crouching, close-growing trees that loomed above her.

"Put it in neutral." It was Cody's voice, coming in her side window.

Juliet slowly turned from her close study of the crouching trees to look at him. She was hoping, in a distant sort of way, that he might have grown ugly or something, that her heart wouldn't start its rapid, anticipatory pounding at the sight of him.

But her hopes were dashed. He was more beautiful than ever, and her silly heart was jumping around in her chest just like it always did lately.

"Did you hear what I said?" he demanded.

"No. No, I guess not."

"Damn it, Julie." He spoke gruffly. "We have to get this car out of the middle of the road. It's not safe."

"Oh." That made sense. "Yes. Of course."

"Shift into neutral and steer. I'll push."

She nodded. "Certainly. I will." She shifted, and then gave him a numb smile.

"Fine," he said, looking put out. "Now steer."

He got behind the car and pushed, while she steered the car to the side of the road in front of his pickup. Then she conscientiously set the parking brake.

"Flip the hood latch," he told her then.

She did as he instructed. He opened the hood and poked around in there with a flashlight he must have brought from his pickup. Finally, leaving the hood up, he came back to her side of the car.

"Well?" she asked.

"It's bad," he told her.

"How bad?"

"You've thrown a rod. Basically, your engine's blown."

"My engine?"

"Yeah. The truth is it'll probably cost you more to fix this piece of junk than the thing is worth now."

Something gave inside of Juliet then. Her spirit seemed to break. It was only a car—she knew that. But in a way, it also represented all the changes she'd made in her life. All the changes that had, one by one, gone sour.

Midsummer Madness was truly over. Real life loomed. She and Cody were through. She'd probably have to move out of the guesthouse soon, say goodbye to Black Bart and

Lucky and Kemo. And she'd have to buy a new car, a dependable car. Something brown, with four doors.

Cody was standing right beside her, so she couldn't get out. And she wanted to get out. She said very politely, "Excuse me, Cody."

He looked at her a little strangely, but he did step back. She got out of the car and closed the door behind her. "Thank you," she said to him, "for, um, pushing the car to the side, and for looking under the hood, and everything."

"Julie?" He was really giving her a deep look now. "Julie, are you all right?"

"Fine. Just fine. I just want to get started back, that's all."

"Back where?"

"Home. To town." He kept looking at her as if she wasn't making sense. And maybe she wasn't. What did it matter? She didn't have to make sense to him; they were through. She waved a hand in front of her face. "I'm going back, that's all," she told him. "Just back." She pointed down the dark road in the direction they had come. "That way."

She turned then, with great dignity, and began walking down the highway, into the dark heart of the night.

Eleven

Cody stared after her as she walked away. Her slim back was very straight, her head high. She walked a little stiffly on those high-heeled shoes.

"Julie!" he called after a moment, as the total absurdity of what she was doing sank in. Was she planning to walk the fifteen miles to town in pitch darkness? That would be insane. "Julie, stop!"

She didn't even pause. She kept on walking. Soon she'd turn the bend and the darkness would swallow her; she'd be lost to his sight.

"Julie!"

She turned the bend.

Cody stood there, staring after her, watching the place where her scarlet dress had vanished—and understood how completely his plot to give her a taste of her own medicine had backfired. He felt a healthy surge of shame.

Hell, he realized, he didn't know a damn thing about working out problems with a woman. He'd never had to work when it came to women. They chased him, and he said yes to the ones he wanted. And if a woman left him, he always knew another would be along soon enough.

But there would never be another Julie—he knew that. He was desperate not to lose her, yet right now she was walking into the night, away from him.

Something was really bothering her. And instead of keeping after her to find out exactly what, he'd thrown up his hands and walked out on her, decided without asking her that she must be dumping him—and then tormented her all day.

Even in the darkness, he'd noticed that her eyes were red-rimmed from crying. Right now, she was probably thinking he could care less about her—when nothing could be further from the truth.

They had to talk, damn it. Now, tonight, as she'd always promised they would. But first he had to catch up with her.

"Julie!" he shouted out loud.

And then he took off at a run for the turn where she'd vanished.

Juliet heard him coming. He was pretty hard to tune out.

And the knowledge that he was coming after her pushed back the numbness a little. That was bad, because when the numbness went away, the tears returned. She could feel them, closing off her throat, blurring her sight—which was pretty minimal anyway, in the pitch darkness along the road.

"Julie, wait! Please, Julie...."

He was catching up to her. His voice was closer now. The tears spilled down her cheeks. She hated her own tears and didn't want him to see her cry.

Irrational now, frantic to get away, to salvage some scrap of pride at least, she began to run. It was a stilted, hobbled flight because of her impractical high heels.

"Julie, wait!"

She turned, saw him, a shadow looming ever nearer. She veered off the road and into the dense growth of the trees.

"Julie, stop!"

She tried to run faster, stumbling and tripping, feeling her way around the looming shapes of the trees.

But it was no use. He was right behind her, calling for her. She sobbed and stumbled on a rock, lifted her other foot to catch herself, and it caught on an exposed root. She pitched forward with a little scream, and felt her ankle turn, heard a gruesome cracking sound as something happened to the bone.

Pain sliced up her leg, like a knife slashing from the inside. She landed on the hard ground, moaning, and somehow managed to reach out and free her foot, though she nearly passed out from the pain when she did so.

There was, she realized dimly through the pain, a tree trunk behind her; she'd landed against it. She dropped her head back on the rough bark, her eyes pressed shut in agony, her breath coming in quick, frantic pants.

"Julie?"

She peered up, through the darkness, to see his dim face.

He dropped to his knees before her. "What is it? Your leg?" He reached for her injured ankle.

She let out a scream that was barely human. He jerked back.

And she shouted at him, as she'd never in her life shouted at anyone, "Get away from me! Leave me alone. You've already broken my heart. Isn't that enough?"

After that, there was silence, except for the labored sounds of her breathing and his. He remained, a shadowed shape, kneeling there not three feet away.

As the moments stretched out and the throbbing in her ankle became a mean, insistent agony, Juliet found she was perversely grateful for the pain. It more or less absorbed all her energy, took her mind off everything else.

Cody said softly, "Can you walk on it?"

"No." She bit her lip. "I'm pretty sure it's broken."

"I'll carry you, then."

He moved—slowly, like a man afraid of spooking a skittish animal—to her side. Then he slipped an arm behind her and one beneath her knees. She let out a low groan when he stood up.

"Easy, sweetheart," he crooned.

Juliet twined her arms around his neck and buried her head against his chest, soothed in an elemental way by the solid strength of him. He carried her back to the road and from there to his truck.

At Gap Memorial, her ankle was x-rayed and set. Cody, who hovered so close that the doctor had to ask him more than once to step back, was finally instructed to wait in the lounge. He went unwillingly, reminding a pale but staunch Juliet that he was there if she needed him.

It occurred to him, as he sat on an olive-green plastic couch across from a wild-eyed fellow who jumped every time the swinging doors to the main part of the hospital moved, that the cast and crew of the revue might become worried if he and Julie didn't show up. So Cody placed a call to Jake and told him that Juliet had tripped and broken her ankle.

After that, he sat and waited. And he thought about what she'd yelled at him out there in the woods.

You've already broken my heart. That was what she'd said. But how could he do that . . . unless she loved him?

Did Julie love him?

At the thought, Cody shot up from the plastic couch causing the wild-eyed man to jerk upright and let loose a frightened, wordless shout.

"Sorry," Cody murmured.

"It's okay," the man growled, and then subsided in his chair.

Cody paced back and forth on the linoleum floor. My God, he thought. Did Julie love him? And if she did, why all the suffering and moping around over the past few days?

Unless she thought he didn't love her. . . .

Could that be it? Did Julie think he didn't love her?

Hell, come to think of it, *did* he love Julie? Was that what it was, what *she* was to him? The woman he loved?

The idea was novel to Cody. He just hadn't thought about *love* before.

He felt like she was part of him. He couldn't picture waking up in the morning without her beside him. He wanted to do what he could to help her lead a happy life— with him in it.

Was that love?

He stopped in midstride in his pacing, right in front of the wild-eyed man, who looked up at him warily. "You all right, buddy?" the man asked.

"Yeah." Cody looked down at him. The poor guy was a wreck, eyes bloodshot, hair standing on end. "What happened to you?"

"My wife's in there. Having our first. I passed out. They said I couldn't stay."

"Tough break," Cody sympathized. Since the man was there and looking at him, he then asked, "You know what love is?"

The man swallowed. "You don't ask the easy ones, do you?"

Just then a nurse poked her head in through the swinging doors to the functional side of the small hospital. "Mr. Hickleby?"

The expectant father jumped out of his chair. "Yeah? What? Is she okay?"

"Your wife is fine. You have a healthy baby girl. Follow me, please...."

"Oh my God, a girl. I have a girl." The man grabbed Cody's hand and pumped it heartily. He beamed. "Evelyn is fine."

"Great," Cody said. "Congratulations."

"Yeah, thanks. Gotta go." Wearing a dazed ear-to-ear grin, Mr. Hickleby followed the nurse through the doors.

And Cody sat and waited for Juliet and wondered about the meaning of love.

Eventually they rolled her out in a wheelchair. Her injured leg was stuck out in front of her, covered with a cast from midcalf to her toes.

She looked pale, but peaceful.

"Julie!"

She smiled up at him benignly. "Oh, Cody. There you are." She shifted her glance back over her head, to the orderly who was wheeling her. "It's Cody," she explained. "Cody always saves me. Forever and ever. Whenever I get in trouble. He's my hero, ever since we were kids."

Cody realized they must have given Julie something for the pain—something that had improved her attitude immensely. She blithely signed the papers the admissions clerk presented on a clipboard, and then Cody led the way to his pickup, with the orderly pushing Julie behind him.

He lifted her inside himself, signed for the rental of a wheelchair and crutches and then saw to the stowing of them in the bed behind the cab.

All the way to the ranch, Cody planned what he would say when they got to his place. He wanted to talk about this thing called love. He wanted to tell her all she meant to him, make her understand that without her there was a big hole in his life—a hole he hadn't known was there until she filled it.

Juliet, smiling blissfully, stared out the window and sang that song that had been playing on her tape deck when her car broke down—the one about the woman who had legs and knew how to use them.

When they reached the gate to his house, he swung in, tensing as he realized that she might insist he take her to her place. But he forgot all about how he'd deal with it if she refused to talk to him, because the wide, long driveway was packed with cars.

Julie stopped singing long enough to remark, "Hmm. Company."

All the downstairs lights were on. Kemo wasn't on the porch where he was supposed to be, ready to ward off intruders.

Swearing under his breath, Cody managed to ease the pickup around the other cars. By the garage, he turned it around and then stopped alongside the front of the porch facing the gate, so her door was nearest the house.

The door opened, and Bud Southey came out on the porch.

"What the hell is this?" Cody remarked.

Juliet went on humming her song.

Cody went around to her side, scooped her up against his chest and carried her up the steps. When he reached Bud, the caretaker started explaining, "I didn't know what else o do, Mr. McIntyre. The dog woke me from a sound sleep and when I went out to see what was going on, they were all sitting in their cars, afraid to come out with the dog growling at them and all. I got Miss Oakleaf to roll down her window and she explained about Miss Huddleston. I figured you would probably want me to let them in, because they said they'd wait on the porch otherwise.''

"Great," Cody muttered trenchantly, still cradling a humming Juliet against his chest. He reached the door and kicked it back.

He stepped over the threshold. There, in the living room, sat his dog, happily panting, surrounded by most of the cast and crew of the Midsummer Madness Revue, not to mention all of Juliet's committee heads.

Andrea Oakleaf sprang forward, clucking, giving orders right and left. "Well, here she is. Don't just stand there... Cody, did you bring a chair for her?"

"Uh, in the pickup."

Andrea glanced at Jake, who was up and out the door in seconds flat. He brought it right in and opened it up. Cody lowered Juliet into it.

"We won't stay long," Babe Allen promised.

Melda added, "We just wanted to see that she was okay...."

"Why, she's been drugged," Andrea declared.

Juliet held up two fingers, smiling. "Two little white pills. I feel just fine."

Cody stood back as they surrounded her. Jake produced a present, one that he explained she was to have received at the party, had she managed to make it there. She peeled back the bright paper and opened the box, then brought out a china figurine of a small boy holding a lamb. Even Cody, who wasn't much on figurines, thought it charming.

She held it up, her eyes alight with more than the effect of her two little white pills. "Cody, look. My favorite Hummel. The shepherd boy and the lamb."

He smiled and nodded, as Babe explained that they'd kept it back at the raffle when Juliet said she liked it best. Julie thanked them all. And then Andrea produced one more gift—a brass plaque inscribed To Our Fearless Leader. Babe explained that it was to commemorate Juliet's first—of many—years of directorship of the Midsummer Madness Festival.

Juliet kissed it, proclaimed it wonderful and reached out to everyone for a hug and a peck on the cheek. Cody remained on the sidelines, watching, remembering a shy mouse who had asked him a month ago if she could run Midsummer Madness this year.

At last, everyone admitted it was time to go. Cody saw them to the door, listening patiently to Andrea's admonitions that he take proper care of Juliet, see that she got plenty of rest and nourishing food.

"I promise," he said. "Good night." He shut the door.

Relieved, he turned back to the living room. The moment had finally come when he and Julie were alone. All the things he planned to say chased each other through his head. He wanted to say this just right, he wanted to make it clear to her how it was for him, what they might have together, all they might share.

"Julie..." he began. And then said no more. She was asleep in her chair against the far wall near the fireplace.

Cody sighed. Then he propped a pillow behind her head and draped a light blanket over her lap. After that, he stretched out on the longest end of the sectional sofa to be there when she woke.

*   *   *

"Cody?"

Her soft voice reached him through his dreams. "Um? Yeah? What?"

"Cody..."

He opened an eye. Around the edges of the closed shutters, dawn light shone. He groaned a little, from sleeping in a cramped position on the too-short sofa. And then he pulled himself to a sitting position and raked his hair back with his hands.

He remembered. Julie. She'd been hurt. If it was morning, that meant her medication had probably worn off. He peered across the room, where she sat in the wheelchair, awake now, looking at him.

He jumped up. "They gave me your pills. I left them in the glove box. Are you hurting? I'll get you a couple."

"No." She stretched out a hand. "Wait."

"But, Julie—"

"Please. Come here."

He went to her, took the offered hand. It was slim and smooth in his. He wanted to hold it forever.

Close up, he could see the strain in her face. "You're hurting," he said. "Let me—"

She held tighter to his hand as he tried to leave her side, pulling him back. "No. In a few minutes. First, I want to talk. Now. While my head's clear."

"We can talk later."

She gave a low chuckle. "Later's finally here, Cody. It doesn't hurt that much. And I want to talk more than I want to wipe out the pain."

"All right," he said, and dropped into a chair beside her, one close enough that he could keep hold of her hand. "Can I talk first?"

She looked at him levelly, her expression somewhat grim. "Okay. If you want." He was reasonably sure then that she more or less expected bad news.

He began. "I love you, and I want to marry you. Will you? Marry me, I mean?"

Her mouth dropped open. She swallowed. "What?"

He repeated himself. This time, he thought, with more feeling. "I love you, Julie. Please marry me."

"You . . . you want to marry me?"

He grinned. "You bet."

"But I thought—" she sputtered.

"You should have *asked*," he advised.

She confessed, "I was afraid. . . ."

He understood. "I know the feeling."

"Oh, Cody. . . ." She reached out her other hand.

He stood and scooped her up and sat back down with her across his lap. His lips found hers. The kiss went on and on and Cody began to think about how they both had too many clothes on.

Then he remembered that her ankle was broken and giving her pain. Reluctantly, he ended the kiss. "Now I'll get those pills."

She clutched his shoulders. "Wait. In a minute. There's something I want to say. I want you to understand, I want to tell you . . . how it's been for me."

He sat still. "Okay. Go ahead."

She fiddled with a button on his shirt. "I love you, too."

"Good."

"And I've known it since the first night, when we made love. But I couldn't bring myself to tell you because I was sure I was going to lose you to another woman someday, someone like the redhead at the ball, someone more beautiful, more sophisticated—more *everything* than me. I guess that's why I pushed you into her arms for the last dance. Some confused part of me reasoned that since I was going to lose you anyway, I might as well get it over with.''

He tried to speak. She put a finger on his lips. "Shh. Let me finish. I've spent thirty years of my life feeling like the invisible woman, Cody. It always seemed to me that other people—including men—never even knew I was there. And now I've made some changes, and people are taking notice. But I suppose a part of me is still expecting to wake up in the morning and have everybody—including you—looking right through me again.''

He laughed at the impossibility of that and kissed the top of her head. She burrowed in close to his heart. "But I realized last night,'' she said against his chest, "that my fears were only in my head. I couldn't help but see it, the way everyone turned up here, just to be sure that I was all right. I was so grateful, Cody. And a little ashamed that I'd had so little faith in myself and in them.'' She added softly, "And in you, too.''

"I did act like a jerk,'' he confessed.

She chuckled. "You, who've always made it a point *not* to act like a jerk.''

"Love caught me unprepared. But I'll do better. Give me forty or fifty years—the next forty or fifty years. Okay?''

She kissed him. "Could we just make it an even lifetime and leave it at that?''

"Agreed,'' he said gruffly. Then he took her by the shoulders and held her away enough that she had to look at him. "And now I have something I want *you* to understand.''

She looked a little apprehensive. "What?''

He said with great care, "I'm not looking through you, sweetheart. And I'm not looking at any other woman, either. I am now blind to every woman but you. I knew that the first night I kissed you, out there on the porch. But I was too stunned by what you did to me to get the words out then. I'll never look through you again, Juliet Huddleston. You're all the woman I ever wanted to see. Call it love, call it whatever you want. But as far as I'm concerned, there isn't and never will be any other woman for me."

Her eyes looked very soft. "It's true? You really mean that?"

"I do. With all my heart."

She sighed and snuggled close to him, oblivious to the throbbing in her ankle, to her rumbling stomach that wanted breakfast soon, to everything but the feel of Cody's arms around her.

"Oh, Cody." She sighed. "It's like a dream. Me and you."

He chuckled. "More than a fantasy, you mean?"

"Absolutely. It's a dream to last a lifetime. And we've made it real." She lifted her mouth for another lingering kiss.

Out by the barn, Black Bart crowed. Kemo, on the floor, thumped his tail and yawned. Midsummer Madness was over for another year. But for Juliet and Cody, a lifetime of happiness had only begun.

*   *   *   *   *

SILHOUETTE® Desire™

COMING NEXT MONTH

#733 THE CASE OF THE MISSING SECRETARY—Diana Palmer
MOST WANTED
Logan Deverell disliked disruption of his orderly life. But when
secretary Kit Morris decided this bear had been left in hibernation too
long, suddenly calm turned to chaos!

#734 LOVE TEXAS STYLE!—Annette Broadrick
SONS OF TEXAS
Allison Alvarez didn't need any help raising her son, especially not
from rugged businessman Cole Callaway—the man who had turned
his back on her and her baby fifteen long years ago....

#735 DOUBLECROSS—Mary Maxwell
Secret agent Travis Cross was hunting a murderer. But while hiding
out with sexy schoolteacher Alexis Wright, he caught a case of the
chicken pox, and the prescription was love!

#736 HELD HOSTAGE—Jean Barrett
When timid Regan MacLeod was stranded in the snowy wilderness
with accused murderer Adam Fuller, she knew survival depended on
trusting the handsome, bitter man—that and body heat....

#737 UNTOUCHED BY MAN—Laura Leone
As far as scholarly Clowance Masterson was concerned,
Michael O'Grady was a disreputable swindler. But the more time they
spent together, the more she fell prey to his seductive charm....

#738 NAVARRONE—Helen R. Myers
September's *Man of the Month*, Navarrone Santee, had only one
priority—proving his longtime enemy was a brutal killer. But his
efforts were blocked by sultry Dr. Erin Hayes.

AVAILABLE NOW:

#727 AND BABY MAKES PERFECT
Mary Lynn Baxter

#728 JUST LIKE OLD TIMES
Jennifer Greene

#729 MIDSUMMER MADNESS
Christine Rimmer

#730 SARAH AND THE STRANGER
Shawna Delacorte

#731 A RESTLESS MAN
Lass Small

#732 CONVENIENT HUSBAND
Joan Hohl

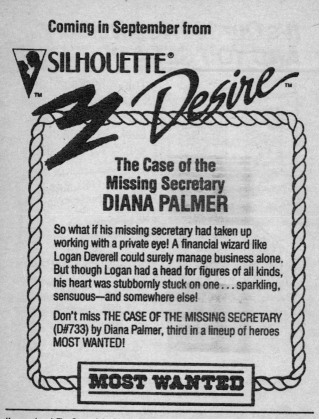